THE BABYSITTERS REMEMBER

Ann M. Martin

Hippo

This book is for
Jahnna and Malcolm,
Dash and Skye

Scholastic Children's Books,
Scholastic Publications Ltd,
7-9 Pratt Street, London NW1 0AE, UK

Scholastic Inc.,
555 Broadway, New York, NY 10012-3999, USA

Scholastic Canada Ltd,
123 Newkirk Road, Richmond Hill,
Ontario, Canada L4C 3G5

Ashton Scholastic Pty Ltd,
P O Box 579, Gosford, New South Wales,
Australia

Ashton Scholastic Ltd,
Private Bag 92801, Penrose, Auckland,
New Zealand

First published in the US by Scholastic Inc., 1994
First published in the UK by Scholastic Publications Ltd, 1995

Text copyright © Ann M. Martin, 1994
THE BABYSITTERS CLUB is a trademark of Scholastic Inc.

ISBN 0 590 55910 9

Typeset by Contour Typesetters, Southall, London
Printed by Cox & Wyman Ltd, Reading, Berks

10 9 8 7 6 5 4 3 2 1

What I Did This Summer
by Kristy Thomas

This summer I did a lot of baby-sitting. My friend Bart and I coached a couple of softball teams for little kids. My friend Mary Anne and I took a marathon bike ride. And my brother

Kristy

Boy, does this sound boring. You know what's wrong with an essay like this? Not only is it dull (even the title is dull), but how could I possibly write about all the things I did this summer? Okay, let's say the summer holiday is eleven weeks long. That's seventy-seven days, which is 1,848 hours or 110,880 minutes. A lot can happen in 110,880 minutes. How could I cram it into a two-page essay? I couldn't. At least not in any great detail, and I do think great details are what make writing worth reading. Nevertheless, this was the assignment given to every single student at Stoneybrook Middle School on the day before the summer holiday began: by the end of the holiday, write a two-page essay entitled *What I Did This Summer*. After hearing that, I almost considered a teaching career myself, just so I could set essays with titles such as *What Happened When I Woke Up This Morning and Discovered I Was the Last Person on Earth*. I would not assign a length for it. If my students wanted to write ten pages, that would be fine. If someone thought they could tell a great story in a paragraph, that would be okay, too.

But I digress.

What I started to say was I knew that by the end of the summer I couldn't tell you what I had done during it in just two pages. I couldn't even tell you what happened last night in two pages. Oh, well. So I'll tell you in more pages, because what happened last night was pretty interesting.

I held a slumber party. Now I've been to an awful lot of slumber parties in my day, but never any that led to what this one led to. The guests were my friends in the Babysitters Club (also known as the BSC): Mary Anne Spier, Stacey McGill, Claudia Kishi, Jessi Ramsey, Mallory Pike, and Shannon Kilbourne. (Two other club members couldn't attend, but I think they were there in spirit.)

My friends started to arrive around dinnertime. Everyone just kind of trickled in, dragging along sleeping bags and overnight bags. Mal was barefoot. Claudia was wearing her bikini top instead of a shirt. Not only was it a stuffy hot day, but we were deep in the middle of the summer holiday and feeling pretty relaxed and casual.

By six-thirty, everyone had arrived. When I was younger, I used to spirit my slumber party guests away to my bedroom the second they showed up, as if my family might contaminate them. But I'm older now, and mature enough to appreciate my big jumble of a family: brothers, stepbrother, stepsister, adopted sister, mum, stepdad, grandmother, and assorted pets. The members of the BSC like my family, too.

So my friends and I ate dinner with my family. We had a picnic in the back garden, complete with a watermelon seed-spitting contest, a marshmallow toast, and, later, firefly catching.

3

(Mary Anne made the little kids let the fire-flies loose before we finally went inside for the night.)

It wasn't until later—after the younger kids were in bed and the kitchen had been cleaned up and the house had grown quiet—that Mallory mentioned the school assignment. I think most of us had forgotten about it (except for Shannon, who doesn't go to our school, so she didn't know about it in the first place).

"The essay," said Claudia with a groan. "Why did you bring that up, Mal? I was *enjoying* the evening."

Mal shrugged. "I don't know. I was thinking about it today. I've been keeping a list of things that have happened, so I can put them in the essay later. I'm rather looking forward to writing it."

Claudia sighed. "It's really a shame," she said.

"What's a shame?" asked Jessi.

"That Mal's such a dork."

A moment of silence followed this statement. Then Mal exclaimed, "Hey! I'm not a dork!" She paused. "Am I?"

"Oh, no. Of *course* not," said Mary Anne, jumping to her feet. But the rest of us burst out laughing. We knew both Claud and Mal were kidding. Mary Anne realized it a moment later, and began to laugh, too. She can be so serious. But she's also very compassionate.

When our giggles died down, we heard a knock

at the door. At least, we thought we did. It was an awfully soft knock.

"Come in?" I said.

The door eased open a couple of centimetres and Karen stuck her head in the room. Karen Brewer is my stepsister. She's seven. She and her brother Andrew live here with their father and my family half the time (alternate months; this is a new arrangement and we like it, even if it takes some adjusting to). The other half of the time they live with their mum.

"Hi, Karen," I said.

"Hi," she replied. "What are you lot doing in here? I heard laughing."

"We're being very silly," Mary Anne told her. "Did we wake you up?"

"Who, me? I wasn't even asleep yet."

I looked at Karen's crumpled nightie and messy hair. Then I checked my watch. I reckoned she'd been asleep for almost an hour.

"Come on," I said. "I'll take you back to your room."

I put Karen in her bed, then returned to my own room. "We'd better be quiet," I said to my friends. "I'm surprised Mum or Nannie hasn't come charging upstairs yet to find out what's going on."

Shannon giggled. "I can't imagine Nannie actually charging anywhere," she said. "She's too—" Shannon paused mid-sentence.

"Too old?" I supplied. (Nannie is my grand-mother, and to me she doesn't seem too old for anything.)

"Oh . . . no," said Shannon. "I—I meant—"

"You can't dig yourself out of this one," said Stacey gleefully.

"Oh, well." Shannon was blushing. Then she made a monumental effort to unblush, grabbed a pillow from my bed, and threw it across the room at Stacey.

Stacey threw it back.

It hit me. The fight was on. Even as I was heaving Mary Anne's stuffed bear (she had actually brought a *teddy* bear to the sleepover) at Jessi, I was calling out, "You lot, we have to stop! I mean it." (A rolled-up pair of socks hit me on the arm.) "I'm not kidding. Mum and—"

The door to my room flew open. There stood Mum, Watson (he's my stepdad, the father of Karen and Andrew), and Nannie.

"Kristy," Watson began, and a T-shirt flew through the room and grazed his forehead.

Every single person in the room fell silent. Finally I said sternly, "Who threw that?"

A squeak escaped from Mary Anne. "I did. I was aiming at you," she whispered.

Watson began to laugh. Mum and Nannie joined him. My friends and I laughed, too, but rather uncertainly.

Finally Mum just said, "Look, if you wake

6

up Emily Michelle, she's your responsibility. Understand?"

Boy, did we. That was all we needed to hear. Emily, my adopted sister (she's from Vietnam), is two and a half. And she's absolutely adorable. Except in the middle of the night when she wakes up and can't go back to sleep. Then she can be up for hours, wanting stories, cups of water, hugs, and who knows what else. I did not want to spend my slumber party helping Emily fall asleep.

"Okay," I said to my friends when the grown-ups had left, closing the door behind them. "We really, really have to be quiet now. We—" I glanced at Mal and saw that she was writing something on a notepad. "What are you doing?" I asked her.

Mal finished writing, capped her pen, snapped the pad shut, and looked up. "I'm just adding this party to my list. My list of things to put in the essay. I'll be sure to include a funny paragraph."

"What *is* this essay you have to write?" Shannon asked.

Stacey rolled her eyes. Then she told Shannon about *What I Did This Summer*. "Can you believe it?" she added.

"Wouldn't you think a bunch of teachers could come up with a more stimulating topic?" I said. "I thought teachers were supposed to encourage creativity. Or at least make you think."

"Right," said Jessi. "How much thought will

go into this essay? All we have to do is list what happened over the summer."

At this, Claudia gasped and pretended to look appalled. "What if . . . *nothing* happened to you?"

Mal was thoughtful. "I don't mind writing this essay," she said, "but I *would* have more fun writing about, I don't know, maybe the happiest day of my life. Now I would really need to think about that."

"What about your most embarrassing moment?" suggested Mary Anne.

"Your most humbling experience," said Shannon.

I think it was Jessi who said, "I know. Your most vivid memory. Not your most im*por*tant memory, but the one that's clearest in your mind."

Hmm. My friends and I settled down. Talk about something that makes you think. I shifted position on my bed. Next to me, Claud and Stacey did the same. Shannon sat cross-legged in my armchair. Mary Anne lay on a sleeping bag, her head propped up on her teddy bear. And Mal and Jessi sat back-to-back on the floor, supporting each other.

"The hard part," I said, "is deciding on your *most* vivid memory. I can remember lots of things, but what do I remember the *most* clearly?"

"I've got it!" said Stacey triumphantly. "The

8

day I—no, wait. *That* isn't the most vivid. This really is hard."

"I know my most embarrassing moment," spoke up Shannon. "It was definitely the time I threw up on my aunt's new Oriental carpet. It happened right after she said to me, 'Are you sure you *can* eat three hamburgers?'"

"That's not embarrassing, it's disgusting!" cried Mary Anne.

"Let's think about our happiest days," said Mallory.

"No, our most humbling experiences," said Claudia.

My friends and I talked for hours. We talked until long after everyone else in the house had fallen asleep. And what we talked about could have filled pages. But it would probably wind up as only a sentence or two in my summer-time essay.

Kristy

1st CHAPTER

Kristy

Saturday

This afternoon I babysat for David Michael, Emily Michelle, Karen, and Andrew. It was a pretty regular afternoon. Nothing unusual happened. I mean, nothing unusual babysitting-wise. We played in the backyard with the hose and sprinklers. We bought Popsicles from the ice-cream van. It was just a nice summer afternoon.

One interesting thing did happen, though. As I was watching David Michael run around the yard, a memory came to me. And I think it just might be my most vivid one. Would any of you be surprised to learn it's a babysitting memory? Probably not. Anyway, it's from about three years ago....

I read over what I had written in the Babysitters Club notebook. That's the book in which my friends and I make notes about every single sitting job we take.

What exactly is the Babysitters Club? It's a business, a successful one, and it was started by Mary Anne, Claudia, Stacey and me, way back at the beginning of seventh grade, when we were twelve. (We're thirteen now.) Actually, the original idea was mine. I got it one day after I watched my mother make about a million phone calls, trying to line up a sitter for David Michael for an afternoon when I couldn't sit for him. (This was in the days before Mum had married Watson, so I barely knew Karen or Andrew, and Mum and my brothers and I lived in a much smaller house.) Anyway, I thought: Wouldn't Mum have an easier time if she could make one phone call and reach a whole bunch of sitters? She'd find a sitter much faster.

So Claud and Mary Anne and Stacey and I, who all loved to babysit, began meeting three times a week (from five-thirty until six on Mondays, Wednesdays, and Fridays) in Claud's bedroom. We let people know we were available to take calls then and line up sitting jobs. Before long, we had more jobs than we could handle by ourselves, so we asked a new member to join: Dawn Schafer. Dawn and her mum and brother had just moved here to Stoneybrook, Connecticut, after her parents got divorced, and she and Mary Anne had become good friends. Guess what. Eventually, they became stepsisters. Dawn's mum married Mary Anne's dad (Mary Anne's mum had died years earlier). Dawn isn't around right now, though. She's in California for a while, where her dad lives, and where she grew up. Despite that, we're still close, and we still consider Dawn a BSC member. She'll return to Connecticut before we know it.

Hmm. I've digressed again.

Let me see. Okay, Dawn had joined the club but we still needed help, so two additional members joined—Jessi Ramsey and Mallory

Pike. Shannon replaced Dawn when Dawn left for California. She and a guy named Logan Bruno (who happens to be Mary Anne's boyfriend) were our associate members, meaning that they didn't have to attend meetings, but they could be called on to take jobs if none of the rest of us was free. (Logan is still an associate.)

So these days our club consists of me (I'm the chairman), Claudia (our vice-chairman), Mary Anne (secretary), Stacey (treasurer), Jessi and Mal (junior officers), Shannon (alternate officer), Logan (associate member), and Dawn (our?). We are nine very different people, but we work well together, and run our club professionally.

As chairman, I'm responsible for coming up with great ideas, and for running the club efficiently and effectively. Some of my great ideas are the club notebook I just mentioned, and Kid-Kits. Nobody except Mal, who wants to become an author, truly likes writing in the notebook (well, I don't mind much). My friends think it's a pain. *But*—they have to admit it's a great sitting tool. We're each supposed to read it once a week, and in it we find out about the kids and the families for whom we're sitting. It's always best to be prepared. Kid-Kits are just cardboard boxes that we've decorated and filled with our old toys, books, and games, as well as activity books and art supplies. Kids *love* to see us sitters turn up with

16

the Kid-Kits. Such a simple (but great) idea, if I do say so myself.

I don't know why I'm so good with kids, but I always have been. And I've always enjoyed kids. You would think I grew up in a family with a million younger brothers and sisters (like Mallory's), but that's not so. I grew up with my mum, my two elder brothers Charlie and Sam (they're seventeen and fifteen now), and just one little brother, David Michael, who's seven now. My dad walked out on our family when I was six, not long after David Michael was born. For years, Mum worked hard to build her career and bring up my brothers and me. (I think she did a terrific job.) She didn't meet Watson until I was in seventh grade. By the summer, they were married, and my entire life changed. I moved from the house in which I'd grown up (across the street from Claudia and next door to Mary Anne) to Watson's mansion. (Watson is really rich.) I acquired my stepsister and stepbrother. Then Mum and Watson adopted Emily, and then Nannie moved in to help run our growing household. This household, by the way, also includes Shannon the puppy (named after Shannon Kilbourne who gave him to us), Boo-Boo the cat, Goldfishie and Crystal Light the goldfishes, and (whenever Karen and Andrew are with us) Emily Junior the rat and Bob the hermit crab. I need a computer to keep track of all of us—but I wouldn't swap this life for the world.

As you might be able to tell, I am outspoken and energetic and full of ideas. Some people say I'm bossy and have a big mouth. (They may be right.) So guess who my best friend is? Shy, quiet, sensitive Mary Anne. I think opposites really do attract. Mary Anne, the BSC secretary who's responsible for keeping our record book up-to-date, and scheduling all our sitting jobs, grew up with just her dad. Mr Spier, trying to be both a mother and a father to Mary Anne, wound up treating her pretty strictly. He made lots of rules, and made her wear these little-girl clothes and tie her hair in plaits. Now that he's married to Dawn's mum, though, he's loosened up a lot. Not only has he relaxed the rules, but Mary Anne is allowed to wear much more grown-up outfits, and recently, she even got this very trendy short haircut. (Until then, she and I actually looked quite a bit alike, since we both have brown hair and brown eyes and are on the short side.) More surprisingly, Mr Spier has allowed Mary Anne to have a steady boyfriend. Mary Anne and Logan have been going out since the beginning of eighth grade. They've had their ups and downs, but they're still together. (None of the rest of us has a relationship quite like Mary Anne's with Logan.)

Stacey is our treasurer, responsible for keeping track of our money and collecting our club subs, which she's very good at, since she not only likes maths, but excels at it. Like my parents and Dawn's, Stacey's are divorced. Her mum lives here in Stoneybrook; her dad lives in New York City, which is where Stacey, an only child, grew up. Maybe because of this (growing up in NYC, I mean) Stacey is the most sophisticated person I know. She dresses in *very* trendy clothes, and she's allowed to have her hair permed. Stacey may be pretty and popular and all those enviable (to some people) things, but she has not had it easy. There's the divorce, of course, but even before that, Stacey's doctor made a scary discovery: Stacey has a severe form of diabetes. This is a disorder in which her body doesn't process sugar properly, so Stacey has to help it along. She sticks to a strict no-sweets diet and gives herself daily injections of something called insulin. (I always say I could never do that, and Stacey replies that I could if my life depended on it. She should know.) As long as Stacey eats extra carefully and monitors her blood sugar level, she stays fairly healthy. We keep our fingers crossed. In terms of her personality, Stacey is funny, caring, responsible, likes to have fun, and is a little boy-crazy, although right now she has a boy-friend, and seems only to have eyes for Robert.

Claudia, our vice-chairman, is Stacey's best friend. Although Claud and Mary Anne and I had grown up together and played together, Mary Anne and I were always *the* best friends. I think

Claud felt just a little separate from us. Then Stacey moved here and—bang! Best friendship. Although Stace and Claud don't look at all alike, and they certainly do not agree on what foods to eat, they do have a lot in common. The differences: Claud is Japanese-American with long, long silky jet-black hair and dark almond-shaped eyes, while Stacey has shorter blonde hair and blue eyes. Claud is addicted to junk food and keeps it hidden around her room. (It's hidden because her parents disapprove of such a diet. Frankly, so do I.) Stacey could probably go into a diabetic coma just by standing in that room amid all the sugar. (Well, not really.) On the other hand, Claud is as fashion-conscious as Stacey, although I think she dresses more outrageously. And she is sophisticated and fairly boy-crazy, but currently minus a boyfriend. Several more things about Claud: she lives with her parents and her genius of an older sister Janine (Mimi, her beloved grandmother, died a while ago), she hates school and does poorly at it even though she's clever, and she adores art of any type and is very (I repeat, *very*) talented. She draws, paints, sculpts, and even makes jewellery.

Jessi and Mal, another pair of best friends, are junior officers because they are eleven, two years younger than the rest of us, and not allowed to babysit at night, except for their own brothers and sisters. Jessi grew up in New Jersey and moved to Stoneybrook just when she was beginning sixth grade. She lives with her mum and dad, her aunt Cecelia, her eight-year-old sister Becca, and her baby brother, whose nickname is Squirt. Oh, and their hamster, Misty. Jessi is horse-crazy (like Mal), but that's probably just a passing interest. What's more important is that she's a very (I repeat, *very*) talented ballet dancer. She's taken lessons since she was just a little kid, and now attends a special dance school in nearby Stamford, Connecticut, where she has danced the lead role in a number of productions.

Remember when I said Mal grew up with a million younger brothers and sisters? Well, that wasn't quite true. She grew up with seven. After Mal come ten-year-old identical triplets, Jordan, Adam, and Byron; nine-year-old Vanessa, who wants to be a poet one day; eight-year-old Nicky; seven-year-old Margo; and five-year-old Claire, the baby of the family. You can certainly see how Mal developed her interest in children. I think she's been a second mother in her family for most of her life. As I mentioned, Mal is also horse-crazy, but like Jessi, her true interest lies somewhere else: in writing. Mal is bound and determined to write and illustrate children's books when she grows up. I'm sure she'll be able to. Speaking of growing up, this has been a thorn in Mal's side for as long as I've known her. What she wants most right now is to be *older*, so she can

21

get her brace off and exchange her glasses for contact lenses (which her parents will not allow her to do now). Mal feels like an ugly duckling, with her brace, glasses, and unruly red hair. (But she isn't.) By the way, in terms of looks, Mal and Jessi are about as different as Claud and Stace. Mal is average height, has that red hair, the brace and glasses, and she's white. Jessi is tall with long graceful legs, has dark hair, no brace and only reading glasses, and she's black.

Shannon is currently our alternate officer. (That was Dawn's job, but Shannon has taken it over on a temporary basis. She'll give it up when Dawn returns.) The alternate officer takes on the duties of any club member who can't make it to a meeting. Shannon lives across the road from me at my new house. When I first moved here I thought she was an incredible snob, but now I know she isn't. It took a while, but we became friends, even though we are as different as night and day. One thing I like about Shannon is that she's an animal-lover. So am I. Well, actually, she's just a dog-lover, but that's good enough for me. Shannon's family breeds Bernese mountain dogs, and they gave us Shannon the puppy after our collie Louie died. (David Michael was the one who named Shannon the puppy after Shannon the human.) Another thing I like about Shannon is that she's a very dedicated student. School is one of the most important things in her life, and she works extremely hard. (As I mentioned earlier, Shannon does not attend Stoneybrook Middle School with the rest of us. She goes to Stoneybrook Day School, which is private.) Shannon lives with her parents, her two younger sisters (Tiffany and Maria), and Astrid of Grenville (Shannon the puppy's mother).

The final club member is Logan, Mary Anne's boyfriend and our BSC associate. Logan moved to Stoneybrook from Louisville, Kentucky, with his family (his parents, his younger sister Kerry, and his little brother Hunter) at the beginning of eighth grade. He and Mary Anne fell for each other almost immediately. I can see why Mary Anne likes him. Logan is warm, funny, caring, and he understands Mary Anne. Also, he's cute.

The nine of us are a pretty interesting group. We're such different people, but we work so well together. I think that's one reason the BSC is a success. But the club wouldn't be here in the first place if I hadn't had my great idea. And I probably wouldn't have come up with the great idea if I didn't like to entertain kids so much. And that began with David Michael. Oh, and my mum. She was important, too. . . .

23

2nd CHAPTER

Kristy

When I was ten, my life was pretty different to when I was thirteen and living with Watson in the big house across the road from Shannon Kilbourne. I lived with just Mum and my brothers and our dog Louie then. Charlie was fourteen, Sam was twelve, and David Michael was only four. We went to four different schools. Charlie had just started high school, Sam was in seventh grade at SMS, I was in fifth grade at Stoneybrook Elementary, and David Michael went to this combination day care and preschool.

Even then, I was used to life without my dad. I think we all were. He'd been gone for four years. But Mum's life without Dad wasn't easy. She was responsible for everything—bringing us up, working (Dad never sent any money), and

running the house. I used to look at her sometimes and wonder how she did it. She did have a
little help. As soon as she could afford to, she
hired this housekeeper, Mrs Culp. Mrs Culp was
supposed to come in every day to help with the
cooking and the housework, and also to take care
of David Michael so he wouldn't have to spend all
day in day care. Mum liked him to come home in
the afternoons so he could play with Charlie and
Sam and me. She thought he could have quality
time with his sister and brothers, even if he
couldn't have a lot of quality time with her.

The only thing was, Mrs Culp didn't turn up
half the time.

"Mum, you should hire someone else," I used
to say.

"I can't afford anyone else," she would reply.

It was really too bad that the only housekeeper
Mum could afford was a bad one. On the other
hand, I liked to entertain kids, so when Mrs Culp
was playing truant, and Charlie was in charge
after school, he would let me play games with
David Michael or take him out in the garden.
Sometimes Claudia and Mary Anne would join
me.

Claud lived across the street and Mary Anne
lived next door. Here's the great thing about my
bedroom window. I could look out of it—and
right into Mary Anne's bedroom. We signalled
to each other with torches, and hooked up this

basket that we could slide back and forth on a rope between our windows. We sent each other food and homework assignments and notes.

Every morning, Mary Anne and Claudia and I walked to school together, and every afternoon we walked home together. We had been doing that since kindergarten. (Back then, Janine Kishi was assigned to walk with us, as our guard or something, but by fifth grade we'd been walking by ourselves for several years. Besides, Janine went to SMS by then.) Anyway, it was funny, but for as long as I could remember, Mary Anne and Claudia and I had been friends, a threesome. But Mary Anne and I had always been the *best* friends. As I said, Claudia didn't have a best friend until seventh grade, when Stacey moved to Stoneybrook. Maybe it had something to do with those windows. I always felt that through them, Mary Anne and I could look into each other's lives.

I suppose things were pretty simple then. My days revolved around school, home, homework, my friends, and not much else. Except for one important thing: independence. I always wanted more of it. It seemed that all my life I was trying for the next, more independent step. I couldn't wait to get the stabilizers off my bicycle. As soon as I did, I asked for permission to ride up and down the pavement, and as soon as Mum granted that, I was just *waiting* to be allowed to ride in the road. When I was older, I asked for my own house key. I was extremely relieved when Mum said I could walk to school without Janine—if the Kishis and Mr Spier allowed it. (Mr Spier waited an entire *year* before he allowed it.) And I liked learning how to do things myself. I especially liked learning how to take care of David Michael. I liked to be in charge. (Claudia sometimes called me Miss Boss.)

Here's what nobody understood: I saw my mother doing all these things by *herself* (going to work and taking care of us kids) and I wanted to be just like her. Also, I wanted to help her, which partly explains what happened during the beginning of October in the year I began fifth grade.

It started one morning when Mum was trying to make breakfast, get ready to leave for her office, and hustle my brothers and me off to school. I suppose it was a typical weekday morning.

"Charlie!" Mum hollered. "*Please* feed Louie. He's starving. And he's underfoot. Either feed him, or finish scrambling these eggs. I can't do both."

"Mum, I've lost my homework," said Sam.

"Louie probably ate it," I remarked.

"I have a stomach ache," announced David Michael.

"You have one every morning," said Sam.

"Charlie, where *are* you?" Mum called again.

"Right here," he said, dashing into the kitchen.

"Mum, do you think I need to shave yet?"

"Well, not this morning," she replied. "Kristy, could you put the eggs on the plates, please?"

"Okay . . . Mum, am I old enough to get loafers?"

"No, they're not good for your feet. Wait until sixth grade."

The thing was, I didn't even like loafers; I just wanted to know I was old enough for them in case I changed my mind.

We finally threw breakfast together, and Charlie finally fed Louie. Just as we were sitting down at the table, with Louie chomping and slurping away in the corner, the phone rang.

"Can I answer it?" asked David Michael.

Mum said no. David Michael had no phone manners yet.

"*I'll* get it," I said. I reached for the receiver. I thought Mary Anne might be calling. But it was Mrs Culp. I handed the phone to Mum, passing the cord over Sam's head. And I made a face. An early morning Mrs Culp call was never good news.

Sure enough, Mrs Culp was calling to say she wouldn't be able to make it. She didn't even say why.

"Can't she ever call me the night *before*?" said Mum, as I hung up the phone for her. She let out an enormous sigh. "She never seems to know ahead of time." Then Mum did what she always had to do when Mrs Culp backed out at the last minute. She phoned Mrs Pike to see if she could pick up David Michael at the day care centre after she picked up Nicky Pike from afternoon kindergarten. (When Mrs Culp had been hired, Mum had signed up David Michael only for the 8.00—3.00 programme at the centre.) Then she turned to Sam and Charlie to see which of them was free that afternoon and could be in charge until she came home from her office. "Charlie?" she said.

"Well, I *could*. But I'd have to miss practice."

"Sam?"

"I have, um, detention."

Mum shot him a Look. Then she turned back to Charlie.

Before she could say anything, I burst out, "Mum, what about *me*? I don't need a sitter any more. I can take care of myself. *And* I can take care of David Michael. Please? I'm old enough to. Honest. You know I am. It'll just be for two hours, until Charlie or Sam gets home. I'll *race* home from school. I'll be here before Mrs Pike drops off David Michael. And we can play outside if you don't want us in the house. We'll stay right out in the back. We wouldn't even leave the garden. Please, please, please? You know I'm great with David Michael. *He'd* like it. Wouldn't you, David Michael? Wouldn't you like that?"

29

"What?" David Michael had no idea what was going on.

"Mum?" I said again.

Mum looked at me, then at David Michael, then at Sam, then at Charlie, and then back at me. "Well . . . all right."

I had been ready to protest. I was going to exclaim, "But I *am* old enough. I *am*!" Instead I said, "Are you kidding me?"

Mum smiled. "Nope. You may be in charge of your brother this afternoon. And you don't even have to confine yourselves to the garden. Just don't use the cooker. And don't open the door unless you know who's on the other side of it. And don't—"

"I won't! I promise I won't," I interrupted. "I won't do . . . I won't do any of those things you just said. Also, I won't let David Michael out of my sight. And I'll plan some great games. Or something."

Mum looked at her watch then. It was time to rush off to school. I tore outside, my bookbag banging against my knees, and my house key on its chain thumping against my chest.

"Mary Anne!" I shouted as I ran next door. "Mary Anne!"

Mary Anne dashed down her front steps. (Her father watched her from the doorway. He wouldn't close the door until we had safely crossed the street.) "Good morning," she said. Then she added, "What?"

"*I* am going to babysit for David Michael this afternoon," I told her proudly. "All by myself."

3rd CHAPTER

Kristy

I barely paid attention in school that day. While my teachers talked about long division and peace treaties, I thought up art projects David Michael would like. While my gym teacher gave us soccer drills, I wondered if I could teach David Michael to play hopscotch. Then I began to think of more practical things, such as remembering to take David Michael to the bathroom the minute he came home from school, and not letting him eat sweets before dinnertime.

I drove my reading teacher crazy, but I couldn't help it. Who can concentrate on Paul Bunyan stories when she's facing her first proper babysitting job? I just had to prove I was good at it. This was a giant step towards independence. Mum was going to let me be responsible for—not me, not Louie—*another human being*.

The second the bell rang at the end of the day, I leaped out of my seat. I gathered my things together and raced out of my classroom and down the corridor. If I didn't beat Mrs Pike to my house, I was a dead duck.

"Hey, Kristy! Where are you going?" called Claudia.

I was tearing past the spot where Mary Anne and Claudia and I always waited for each other.

"Home!" I shouted as I shot by her. "I'm in a hurry. See you later!"

I ran every step of the way to my house. I didn't slow down until I was running up the path. When I finally reached the front door, I leaned against it, panting, my heart pounding. Then I pulled the key from around my neck and opened the door.

I had done it. I had beaten my little brother home. So far so good.

I decided to have some food ready for David Michael. I bustled around the kitchen, preparing the healthy snack I had planned during spelling class. Apple slices and crackers with grape juice.

Ring, ring.

I reached for the telephone, trying to remember Mum's safety tips: never tell a caller you're at home alone, don't give out any information, if he asks to speak to a parent tell him I will call him back if he leaves his phone number.

"Hello, Thomas residence," I said. I hoped I sounded like a grown-up.

"Kristy? It's Mrs Newton." (She was a neighbour, so that was safe.) "Did you just get home from school? What are you up to?"

"I'm fixing a snack for David Michael and me. And I've locked the door behind me and I've already put my school things away." (That part wasn't true, but it would be in a few minutes. And I knew—I just *knew*—that Mum had asked Mrs Newton to check up on me.)

"You aren't using the cooker, are you?" asked Mrs Newton.

"Oh, no!" I tried to sound shocked. "I'm not even using the refrigerator." That really was true. The juice carton had been sitting out on a counter.

"Well, okay. Call me if you need anything."

"All right. Thanks. 'Bye, Mrs Newton."

As I was hanging up the phone, I heard a car door slam. I ran to the front window and looked outside. Mrs Pike's car was in the drive, and she was watching David Michael run along our front path.

I opened the door for my brother, waved to Mrs Pike, let David Michael inside, and locked the door behind him.

"Hi!" I said cheerfully. "How was school?"

"Fine."

"Good. Go to the bathroom and then you can have a snack."

"Do I have to go?"

"Yup."

David Michael heaved an enormous sigh. "Okay. But I need my privacy."

I smiled. "I'll wait outside." David Michael had been needing his privacy since he was three. Mum said it was normal.

While I was standing in the hall, the phone rang again.

"Hello, Thomas residence," I said.

"Hi, hon," said Mum's voice. "How are you doing?"

I gave her the rundown. Then I let her talk to David Michael as he emerged from the bathroom. "And he has clean hands," I told her before I passed the phone to my brother.

A few minutes later, David Michael and I sat down at the kitchen table. My brother surveyed the plate in front of him. "Good snack," he said approvingly. He began to munch away.

Of course the phone rang again.

But this time it was Mary Anne. "Can you come over?" she asked.

"Mary *Anne*. I'm *baby*sitting."

"I know. Bring David Michael with you." Mary Anne had this new babysitter of her own, and she didn't like spending entire afternoons with her. The woman was studying to be a

35

beautician and she made Mary Anne read aloud to her from hairdressing manuals while she practised styling wigs that were perched on polystyrene heads.

"I can't. Mum keeps checking up on me. If I didn't answer the phone she'd have a heart attack," I said.

"Then can I come over there?" asked Mary Anne in a small voice.

"I—you'd better not." (I felt horrible.) "I'm sure I'm not supposed to have friends over while I'm babysitting, and I want to do everything perfectly. If I make a single mistake, Mum'll never let me do this again." I honestly did not think I was exaggerating.

Then I heard a voice in the background call to Mary Anne, "Come and help me with these pin curls!"

"I'd better go," said Mary Anne. "See you later."

David Michael had finished his snack by then. "Kristy? Can we go outside? Mummy said we didn't have to stay inside. Didn't she?"

I hesitated. "Yes, but . . ."

"What?"

"I don't know how we can play outside and hear the phone, too."

"Can we leave the door open?"

"No! The screen door doesn't lock. That wouldn't be responsible."

36

"Could we—" David Michael was interrupted when the doorbell rang. "I'll get it!" he shouted. He turned and dashed towards the front door.

I was right on his heels. "We have to see who's there before we open the door," I said.

David Michael peeped out of the window at the doorstep. "Hey, it's Mimi!" he cried.

Mimi, Claudia's grandmother, lived at the Kishis', and everyone loved her. All the kids in the neighbourhood called her Mimi, just like Claudia did. I opened the door. "Hi, Mimi!" I said.

"Hi, Mimi!" added David Michael.

"Hello there," replied Mimi in her careful, slow voice. "How are you getting along? May I help you with anything?"

I grinned. "Oh, no thanks. We're fine."

"We didn't use the cooker," said my brother.

Mimi smiled. "That is wonderful. I am proud of both of you. You are so grown-up. Please phone me if you need anything."

"Thanks, Mimi. 'Bye!" I called.

As soon as I had locked the door again, David Michael said, "Now can we go out?" He looked awfully hopeful.

"Let me think," I replied.

Finally I decided we could play in the back garden after all if we left the door open and closed the screen door. We could keep Louie with

37

us for protection, and we would be able to hear the phone.

You would not believe what happened during the next hour or so. Mrs Newton phoned again. Then Mrs Pike phoned. Then Mum called again. And *then* Mary Anne's babysitter came over to check on us. (Mary Anne was with her. Her hair was in rollers.) Luckily, the sitter left before David Michael fell over, grazed his knee, and cut his hand. By the time Mum came home later, Sam and Charlie had returned, and David Michael's injuries had been cleaned up and bandaged. He was happily gluing together a macaroni sculpture at the picnic table in the garden, when Mum's car pulled into the drive.

"Hi, kids!" she called. "How did you do?"

"We're in one piece," I replied. "So is Louie. So is the house."

Mum was impressed. (I am not bragging. She really was.) She went right inside and did an inspection. She didn't even try to pretend she *wasn't* doing an inspection. She kept walking around saying things like, "Kitchen is clean, good. David Michael had a snack, good. The cooker wasn't used, good. The front door is locked, good. . . . But the back door isn't."

"We kept Louie with us. He guarded the door," I said.

"Hmm. Okay." Mum turned to Sam and Charlie. "Your sister did well."

I beamed.

Guess what Mum did the next day. She fired Mrs Culp. After that, we all had more housekeeping chores, but nobody minded (much). And for the next two years, Sam and Charlie did most of the babysitting. But they didn't mind (much). The point is, my brothers and I were helping Mum. And by the time I turned twelve I knew I was ready to start my very own sitting business.

I had been bitten by the babysitting bug, and I knew I'd be good at it.

Stacey

4th CHAPTER

Stacey

Dear Dad,
   Hi! How's the Big Apple? Stoney-brook is great, but I miss you, and I can't wait for our weekend together.
   Dad, guess what my friends and I did the other night. We had a sleepover at Kristy's. I know, I know. We do that all the time. The interesting thing, though, is what we started talking about. Someone suggested that we each try to think of our most vivid memory. That was harder than it sounds.

Stacey

I remembered a lot of things, good
and bad. But I didn't decide on
the most vivid one until this morning.
Since it has to do with you and
Mum, I thought I'd write to you about it.

My most vivid memory is of a time just two years
ago, when I was eleven. I still lived in New York
City then. My mum and dad weren't having
problems yet. (Well, maybe they were, but I
didn't know about them.) The three of us lived in
a nice apartment on the Upper West Side. I had
never heard of a town called Stoneybrook, or
thought about living in Connecticut. In fact, I
hadn't thought about living anywhere except
New York, which is where I was born. I am a
native New Yorker. (You can't say that about just
anyone.)

One other thing about that time. I had not yet
been diagnosed with diabetes.

I remember the very first day of school that
year. I was beginning sixth grade. I went to a
private school. My very best friend was Laine
Cummings. That year, she was going to be in my
class at school. One of the nice things about being
friends with Laine was that our parents were
friends, too. Our mums were especially close.

This meant that almost every time I said, "Mum, can Laine come over?" or "Can Laine stay the night?" Mum would say yes, because then she could see Mrs Cummings.

Anyway, on that first day of sixth grade, I sat down at the breakfast table and reached for the jug of juice. I planned to eat in a hurry. Laine and I were going to walk to school together, and we wanted to get there early. I liked school a lot, and I had made myself a promise. Sixth grade was going to be my best year ever. I was going to work hard and earn good grades (straight A's, if possible), I was going to try out for the soccer team, I was going to make new friends. (I had a lot of goals.)

I poured a tall glass of juice, downed it, and poured another.

"Take it easy, honey," said Mum.

"I'm so thirsty."

"Probably all those crisps you ate last night."

"Yeah. A whole big bag. I never pig out like that."

"Well, you're a growing girl."

"Who's a growing girl?" asked Dad as he bounced into the kitchen. I do not know if Dad is actually a morning person, but he is a hard worker, and he has always liked going to the office. (Mum used to say, even then, that he spent far too much time there. Eventually, that was one reason for their divorce.)

45

"I am," I replied. "I'm growing like a weed."

"We should measure you, honey," said Mum. "I bet you grew a couple of centimetres over the summer. Let me get the tape."

"Not now," I said. "After school, okay? I don't want to be late meeting Laine."

The funny thing about Laine was that even though we were best friends, I worried about things like making her wait, even for just a few minutes. Laine had a temper. And she liked to be in charge. She was also one of the most popular girls at school.

I gulped down the rest of my breakfast and flew out of the apartment. Laine and I had had to lobby hard to be able to walk to school by ourselves. But we had done it. I dashed past Henry the doorman.

"'Bye!" I called. "See you after school!"

"'Bye, Stacey. Don't do anything I wouldn't do!"

I sprinted to the corner where I was supposed to meet Laine. I saw her sprinting towards me. "Thought I was going to be late!" we said at the same time.

We laughed. Then Laine said, "I wouldn't mind being late for school, though."

"Oh, come on, Laine. School is okay. You have to *make* it that way. I've made a decision. This is going to be my best year ever. You should do the same thing."

"Oh, Stacey, that is pathetic. You sound like our head. 'You can be whatever you want to be.' 'You can change the world.' 'We are all beautiful people.'"

"Well, I believe those things," I replied. I was going to say more, but I didn't want to get into a fight on the first day of school. Not in the best year of my life.

Laine changed the subject. "Marty's not coming back this autumn," she said.

"She *isn't*?" I was surprised. Marty had been part of our group for two years—ever since our group began. Laine had started the group. She got to control who was in it. Two years ago she had decided on me, Deirdre Dunlop, Val Schirmer, Marty Shultis, and Sally ElMeligi. Laine was the leader. "Why isn't Marty coming back?" I asked. Marty had gone away to camp for the whole summer. I had assumed I'd see her again when school started.

Laine shrugged. "She's changing schools." Laine did not seem too upset. But she was thinking about something. Finally she said, "We'll have to replace her."

"What?"

"We'll have to replace Marty. I mean, someone is bound to want to be part of our group, especially now that Marty's gone."

That sounded a little snobby to me, but I didn't say so.

We had passed Seventy-ninth Street. We rounded a corner, and there it was. Parker Academy. The school I had attended for, well, for ever. I never got tired of the sight of its brick front, and the brass plaque that said *Parker Academy* in discreet letters. To me, it felt like home.

All around us, kids were calling and shouting to each other. A lot of us had been to camp or away on holiday and we hadn't seen each other since the last day of school. Now we were back together, for another year. After a while, kids started walking slowly inside. But not Laine and me. We had a rule. The members of the group didn't go inside until we had all arrived. Laine and I sat by a stone pillar and waited for Deirdre, Val, and Sally.

Val showed up first, walking with her sister and brother. They were twins and only first-graders. Val was holding each one by a hand. (She had to wear a backpack in order to accomplish this.) Val handed them over to a first-grade teacher. Then she ran to us. "Hi, you two! Did you hear about Marty?"

"Yup," said Laine and I.

"Can you believe her parents sent her to boarding school?"

"*Board*ing school?" I repeated. Laine hadn't mentioned that. And from the look on her face, I could tell she didn't know herself.

"Are you sure?" said Laine.

Val nodded. "Marty phoned me last night."

"I wonder why she didn't phone me," murmured Laine.

"She'll be going to school in Massachusetts."

"Hey! Hey, everybody!" Sally was running towards us. She was trying to greet us and ignore her brother at the same time. "Did you hear about—"

"Yeah, we heard," said Laine.

"Okay, we can go inside now." That was Deirdre. She was tearing across the street. She made it just as the Walk sign started to blink Don't Walk. And she looked harried. That was because every now and then, Laine gives the last person to arrive a hard time.

But Miss Chardon saved Deirdre. She was standing at the doorway to school, tapping her finger on her watch.

"We'd better go in," I said.

"Saved by the Chardon," Deirdre whispered to me. I stifled a giggle.

"Well, here you are," said Miss Chardon as soon as we had filed past her.

I wondered who she was talking to. I turned around. A girl was trotting up the steps. She was wearing a brand new Parker Academy sweater, and carrying a brand new Parker Academy bookbag. I could tell she was a brand new Parker Academy student.

49

I nudged Deirdre. "New girl," I whispered.

Deirdre and I both looked at the girl. The girl saw us and grinned. I grinned back. I was remembering my goal to make new friends. The day, I decided, was off to a promising start.

By the end of the day, a lot had happened.

I had found out that the new girl was named Allison Ritz, and she was in our grade. I had introduced myself to her at lunch-time. Then I had invited her to sit with my friends and me at lunch. This was against group rules, but I did not care. (Laine did, though.) I liked Allison a lot.

When I returned from school, Mum came after me with the measuring tape, as she had promised. I had grown three centimetres. But a trip to the bathroom scales showed that I had *lost* four pounds.

"No wonder you ate an entire bag of crisps," said Mum. "You're trying to catch up with your height. Your body is saying 'Feed me!' But not junk food. Try pigging out on healthy stuff, okay, sweetie?"

"Okay," I agreed.

Then Deirdre called. "Guess what. My parents said I could have a sleepover on Friday. For the group. Our first party of the year."

"Cool," I said. "Let's invite Allison. Would your parents let you?"

"I guess . . ." Deirdre replied uncertainly. "But I'll have to check with Laine, you know. And she probably isn't going to like it."

5th CHAPTER

Stacey

Deirdre was right. Laine did not like it one bit. She told me so first thing the next morning when we met to walk to school.

"Oh, come on, Laine," I said. "Allison seems really nice. I like her. And she's new. She moved here from Dallas. She doesn't know anyone in New York, let alone at Parker." I took a swig from my juice carton. I was carrying two more with me, since my growth spurt was making me so thirsty. (I was also carrying an extra large—healthy—lunch to take care of those hunger pangs.)

Laine gave me the evil eye. But all she said was, "You'd better stop drinking so much. You're going to get fat." That meant she was tired of talking about Allison and the slumber party. She had given in.

I spent the next few days doing homework, trying to get to know Allison better, and dribbling a ball around my bedroom. Soccer tryouts had not yet been announced, but I wanted to be ready when they were. Also, I was eating like a horse and drinking like a fish (Henry's words, not mine).

By Friday, I was feeling a little funny. Not sick, exactly. Just kind of dizzy and weird. But I was so hungry and thirsty that I thought, How sick could I be? (Usually when I was sick I lost my appetite.) And I was not about to miss the first slumber party of the year. Especially not after I had managed to get Allison invited to it.

After school on Friday, I tried to rest without Mum knowing what I was doing. If she thought I felt funny, she wouldn't let me go to Deirdre's. I lay on my bed. But I wasn't able to rest much. I kept getting up for drinks of water. I wished fervently for the growth spurt to end (even though I did want to be taller).

Late in the afternoon, I gathered together my sleeping bag, my overnight bag, and some cassettes. Mum accompanied me to Deirdre's apartment. She told me this was because I had so much stuff to carry, but the truth was she didn't want me walking those mean city streets alone. If I wanted to be perfectly honest with myself, I had

53

to admit that I was now feeling shaky, so I was glad for her company—up to a point.

When we reached Deirdre's building, I said to Mum, "I can go up by myself. Thanks for walking me over."

"Okay, sweetie. Have fun." Mum stuffed the sleeping bag under my arm.

I took the lift to the eleventh floor, struggled to Deirdre's door, and rang the bell.

Deirdre opened it in a flash. "Hi! You're the first one here!"

"Great," I replied. "Can I have a drink of water?"

Val, Sally, and Laine arrived as a group a few minutes later. Allison showed up about twenty minutes after they did.

"Sorry I'm late," she said breathlessly. "I am never going to learn my way around New York. Mum and my brother and I walked here and we got completely lost. This city is so *big*."

"It just *seems* big, Allie," I said, at the same time as Laine was saying, "You only live eight streets away. And the streets are *num*bered."

Allison looked hurt, but Deirdre stepped in. "Come on, you lot. Put your stuff in my room. You know, I'm not sure there's enough space for all of us to sleep on the floor. I think two people will have to sleep in my bed."

Deirdre chattered away as we followed her down the hall to her room. When we had dumped all our stuff, she said, "Okay, back to the living room. We have to eat dinner out there. Not with my family—Mum said she wouldn't subject us to Miles," (Miles was Deirdre's seven-year-old brother) "but she also said we can't eat pizza in the bedroom."

We trooped back out to the living room where Deirdre called Ernie's Pizza and tried to place an order. "Three large pizzas," she began.

"Three!" exclaimed Laine.

Deirdre cupped her hand over the receiver. "One's for Mum and Dad and Miles," she hissed. She removed her hand. "Okay, one plain, one with—"

"Pepperoni!" shouted Val.

"Extra cheese!" said Sally.

"Sausage!" said Laine.

"Olives!" I cried.

"How about anchovies?" suggested Allison.

"*An*chovies?" repeated Val, Sally, and Laine.

"Is that some weird Texas thing?" asked Laine.

Even Deirdre covered the receiver again long enough to say, "Anchovies? Are you kidding me?"

But I said, "We could get anchovies on, um, two slices."

In the end, that was what we did. When the pizzas arrived, my friends and I ate them in the living room in front of the video, watching some weird old film that Deirdre's father had *promised* we would like, but which, really, we just found weird and old.

I ate three and a half slices of pizza and drank two cans of Pepsi. I felt full afterwards—but just barely.

When the film was about half over, we abandoned it and returned to Deirdre's room. "So who gets the bed?" asked Laine.

"Deirdre should," said Allison. "It's her bed."

"No, two guests should get it. I'm the hostess."

In the end, we drew straws, and Laine and I ended up with the bed. Everyone else spread out their sleeping bags (Deirdre borrowed mine). Then we sat around on the floor and the bed.

"Okay, where are the munchies?" asked Laine.

Deirdre leaped to her feet. "Right here." She was opening the wardrobe.

"Laine, are you really hungry already?" asked Val.

"No," she replied.

But I was.

Deirdre hauled out bags of crisps and pretzels and M&M's. I hated to sound piggy, but I had to ask, "Is there any more lemonade? I'm—I suppose the pizza was really salty or something."

"You probably ate one of Allison's anchovies," muttered Laine.

"Ignore her," I whispered to Allison. And then I did something I wouldn't ordinarily have had

56

the nerve to do. I took Laine by the wrist and yanked her into the hall.

"Hey!" she cried. "What are you doing?"

"You are being so nasty to Allison," I replied, whispering loudly. "Leave her alone. Or be nice to her."

"Which do you want me to do?"

I sighed. "*Laine*."

"Okay, okay."

After that, Laine was nicer to Allison. Not exactly chummy, but I didn't hear any more muttered comments. I was so relieved that I was able to stop worrying about how I felt—and how much I was eating and drinking. My friends and I told Allison stories about Parker Academy. She told us about living in Dallas, even though she had only lived there for two years. (Her family moved around a lot.)

We did not start to feel sleepy until nearly one o'clock. When we did, we brushed aside the empty lemonade cans and crisp packets, and flopped on to the sleeping bags and the bed.

As Laine and I crawled under the covers she said, "You better not touch me with your cold feet tonight."

I giggled. "I won't. And you better not talk in your sleep . . . or I'll record you."

Laine giggled, too. "I won't."

But what happened later that night was much,

much worse than cold feet or silly mumbled words.

I wet the bed.

It was about four o'clock in the morning. I was having this dream about drinking lemonade under a waterfall in the mountains when I heard screams. In the dream I looked around to see who could be destroying the peace of the woods.

"Stacey! Stacey! Oh, yuk! Get up! Get out of this bed!"

Laine was shaking me as she scrambled out of the bed herself.

"What? What is it?" I asked sleepily.

"You wet the bed, that's what!"

I was about to tell Laine she was crazy when I felt the wet spot on the sheets, and then my soaked nightgown.

"Stacey, you *baby*! That is so disgusting." Laine was running down the hall towards the bathroom. Of course, she had woken up everyone in the apartment. My friends sat up in their sleeping bags. Mr and Mrs Dunlop and even Miles stuck their heads in the room. They were all staring at me. In the bathroom, I could hear the shower running.

"Stacey?" said Mrs Dunlop. "Are you okay?"

"She only drank about a thousand cans of lemonade before she went to bed," spoke up Deirdre.

Slowly I climbed out of the damp bed. I felt

dizzy again. "Can I call my parents?" I asked. What I wanted to say was, "STOP STARING AT ME!"

"I'll call them," replied Mrs Dunlop. "Why don't you go into the other bathroom and change into your clothes."

As I left Deirdre's room, I heard Allison whisper unbelievingly to Val, "She *wet* the *bed*. Gross."

In the bathroom I stripped off my clammy nightgown, cleaned up, and put my clothes back on. (In the other bathroom, Laine was *still* showering. If she could make a drama out of something, she would.)

Mum and Dad both came to pick me up.

"'Bye," said Val, Sally, Deirdre, and Allison uncomfortably as I left. (Laine was changing her clothes and didn't bother to come out of the bedroom.)

"Mum," I said as we stepped into the lift, "I don't feel very well."

"I'm sure you don't, honey," she replied. "I know that was embarrassing for you."

But that was not what I had meant.

6th CHAPTER

Stacey

Somehow I fell asleep again that night. In my own bed, of course. And I did not wet it. When I woke up in the morning I thought: things are never going to be the same after this. I don't know how I knew that, but I did. And it was true. I was not just being dramatic like Laine.

And I did not just mean things would never be the same with my friends. I meant with my body, too. I knew something was wrong, really wrong, with it.

But my parents thought something was wrong with my head. They thought wetting the bed meant I had a psychological problem. And as soon as they could—on Monday, in fact—they packed me off to this fancy child psychiatrist.

Oh, how I wished that a child psychiatrist was

actually a child. A child might have understood bed-wetting better than a grown-up. However, Dr Sherman wasn't bad, for an adult.

The first thing he said to me was, "So how did you survive school today?"

Obviously, Mum had told him about the slumber party.

I relaxed enough to tell him that all of my friends—even Allison, who wouldn't have been invited to the slumber party if it hadn't been for me—had ignored me. And they were *not* keeping the bed-wetting a secret.

"I think the whole school knows," I said to Dr Sherman. I reached into my bag and pulled out a can of ginger ale. The bed-wetting had not done a thing to curb my thirst.

Dr Sherman smiled. "Probably not the *whole* school. But I'm sure it feels that way. Stacey, have you ever wet the bed before?"

I froze. No one else had asked me that question. I considered lying. But then I thought, He's a psychiatrist. He'll know if I'm lying, won't he? He must know what signs to look for.

While I was hesitating Dr Sherman said, "I mean has it happened recently? Not when you were a child."

I knew that's what he had meant. I drew in a breath and let it out slowly. "Yes," I admitted.

"When?"

"About two weeks ago. Maybe a week and a

half ago. I didn't tell my parents because I was embarrassed. I'd drunk three cartons of juice before I went to bed. I changed the sheets quietly in the middle of the night. They never knew."

"Stacey, do you always drink this much?" Dr Sherman watched me finish the can and reach for another.

"Not always. Just lately. I'm hungry all the time, too. Mum measured me. I've grown three centimetres. But you know what? I've *lost* weight. This is a weird growth spurt."

"Are you ever dizzy?" asked Dr Sherman.

"Yes."

"Anything else?"

"Mm . . . sometimes I feel weak. I get tired, too."

Dr Sherman nodded. "Is your mother waiting outside?"

"Yes."

"Okay. Let's call her in."

And that was when Dr Sherman said five awful words. He said them to Mum: "I think Stacey has diabetes." Then he recommended that I see my doctor as soon as possible. And he didn't mean in the next week or so. He meant that afternoon.

Mum took him seriously. She stood right there in his office and called my doctor—even though it was already half past four. The receptionist answered the phone. When Mum couldn't make

Stacey

him understand what was going on, she handed
the phone to Dr Sherman.

Two weeks later I was a different person. At least,
that's how I felt. I had seen my doctor and he had
diagnosed me with diabetes, I had been in the
hospital, I had a new doctor (Dr Werner) who was
a specialist, and I was learning how to give myself
injections of insulin. (Oh, by the way—I did not
need to see Dr Sherman any more, although he
had said I could come back any time I wanted to
talk.)

I was learning a lot of other things, too. For
instance, I was learning what diabetes was and
what it meant. In simple terms, diabetes meant
that my body, for some reason, had become
unable to do something it used to do perfectly
well. It could no longer produce enough of a
hormone called insulin. What insulin does is
regulate the sugar in a person's blood. Without
insulin, sugars and starches build up in the blood
and make you ill. There are different kinds of
diabetes and different ways to take care of it.
Some people can control the sugar in their blood
just by watching what they eat. Other people, like
me, have to watch what they eat *and* give
themselves injections of insulin every day. This
can be tricky—trying to regulate just the right
amount of insulin so you don't have too much or
too little in your blood. You might have to watch

63

your calorie intake, too, be careful to eat certain amounts of things at certain times of the day, and test your blood every so often to make sure you're okay.

As you can imagine, I became pretty used to poking myself with various things, which was a miracle, considering that before this I couldn't even stand to have a flu injection.

Now, you would think I'd be able to start eating properly, take insulin, check my blood— and then just get on with things. That maybe I could still have, if not my best year ever, then at least a pretty good one. But did that happen? No.

First, I missed football tryouts because I was in the hospital. My parents would never in a million years have let me try out anyway. Next I realized that making new friends was pretty much out of the question. I was right when I told Dr Sherman that every kid at school knew what had happened at Deirdre's party. And guess who told most of them. Allison Ritz. She got a lot of mileage out of the story. In fact, Laine liked her retelling of it so much that she invited Allison to replace Marty in our group. If this sounds like an awkward situation, it wasn't. Because I was barely part of the group myself by then. In the first place, I missed tons of school that year. Second, when I did attend, my so-called friends made it pretty clear that they did not want to be seen with me any more than necessary. Except for

StaceyStacey

LaineLaine. But I think Laine was only nice because
her mum told her she had to be.

Anyway, what had my other sixth-grade goal
been? Oh, yeah. Straight A's. Well, forget that.
Every time I started to catch up with my homework, I landed in the hospital again.

"Why is this happening?" I asked Dr Werner
angrily one day. "I am doing everything you say.
I don't eat sweets, I test myself, I give myself the
right amounts of insulin—and then I get ill and
wind up in hospital. Why?"

Dr Werner had one more bit of bad news for
my parents and me. I wasn't just a diabetic. I was
a brittle diabetic. My disease was harder to
control than most. "But we *will* get it under
control," she promised.

It seemed to take for ever.

And that horrible school year seemed to go on
forever. The kids lost interest in the bedwetting
episode, but half of them started calling me a
hypochondriac when I began to miss so much
school. They said I just wanted attention. Then I
fainted at school. Twice. "See?" they said.

The other half must have thought diabetes is
contagious (which it isn't) because they edged
away from me in the cafeteria, and detoured
around me in the corridors.

Mum and Dad were another problem. They
were never convinced that we were doing enough
to treat me, and they dragged me from one

6565

doctor to another, looking for . . . I'm not sure what. Also, they became completely overprotective. They called school every day to see if I was okay. When I was at home, they barely let me out of their sight.

Then, one night in June, Mum and Dad took me out to dinner at a fancy restaurant. Halfway through the meal, Dad made an awkward announcement which I could tell he had rehearsed beforehand.

"Stacey," he said, "your mother and I have made a decision. We are moving to Connecticut. My company wants to transfer me to Stamford, and I said that would be okay. We think the change would be good for you. We know that switching schools will be difficult, but—"

"Dad," I interrupted him, "I cannot *wait* to move to Connecticut. When can we leave?" After my nightmare year, this sounded like a dream. I could start all over again. I could be a new kid somewhere. Somewhere where no one knew about wetting a bed when my best friend was sleeping in it, or fainting in the cafeteria at school, or being a contagious hypochondriac. I made a promise to myself. If I could start all over again, I would not tell a soul about my illness.

And the rest is history. In September I became a student at Stoneybrook Middle School in Stoneybrook, Connecticut. Not long after Claudia Kishi and I fell over each other in the corridor, we became best friends. And I joined the Babysitters Club. Guess what. After all that, *seventh* grade became the best year of my life, although not quite the way I had planned. I got my diabetes pretty much under control. I didn't get straight A's, but I did do well. And I made a whole bunch of good friends. They were such good friends that I could not keep my secret from them—and it did not matter one bit.

Claudia

7th CHAPTER

Claudia

Dear Diary,   Wensday
     I have been think about something
intersting. A few days ago my friends
and I were have a slumbar party and
someone it was Jessy said what is
your most ~~viod~~ ~~vivi~~ your most clear
memory. We all had to think hard.
In fact we cold not deside right
their on the spot most of us are still
thinking. I'am prety sure I have
desided though. My most clear
memory is from when I was six.
That was when I though maybe I
could be an artist one day.

Claudia

I have to go to summer school this year. What a shock. This diary is one of our assignments. We're supposed to write in it every day. Our teacher did not say we have to date our entries or write "Dear Diary," but I do because those things take up space. They make my diary look longer. I was kind of glad that Jessi had posed that question at Kristy's party. It gave me something to write about just when I was running out of ideas. . . .

When I was six I lived in the same house on Bradford Court that I live in now. I lived there with my mum and my dad, my grandmother Mimi, and Janine, my big sister. Janine was nine then. I was in first grade. She was in fourth. I was just beginning to read (and learning veeerrry slooowly). Janine was reading *every*thing. Her teachers even gave her middle school stuff to work on. And they let her enter her science project in the middle school's science fair. I never understood what that project was about. Something to do with energy and electricity and motors.

I did not have a best friend. I didn't have one until I was twelve and Stacey moved to Stoneybrook. I was not unhappy, though. Especially not when I was at home. At home I had Mimi, and my crayons. My beautiful box of sixty-four Crayola crayons with a sharpener in the back. It was not my first box. It was not an old box. It was a new one, the second one Mimi had bought for me since first grade started. I used up box after box. I hardly ever sat in front of the TV set. If I wasn't playing with Mary Anne and Kristy, I was colouring or painting or drawing. Our refrigerator was covered with my pictures. I had done so many they were stuck to it in layers. New ones went up over old ones. Sometimes the magnets could not hold them up any more. Then the pictures fluttered to the floor.

Mimi loved my pictures.

I think Mum and Dad did, too. But they were more interested in how I was doing in school. Which was not very well. They must have been surprised. I mean, after Janine. And school was not a happy place for me. I liked being at home with my crayons. I did not like being at school with Mrs Frederickson. She was old and her hair looked strange. Also, she shouted. The shouting made me scared. It made Mary Anne cry. It made Kristy fight. Mrs Frederickson would shout at our class in the morning. Then we would go outside at break and Kristy would get into an argument with somebody. She was always shoving her fists into someone's face and saying, "Want to make something of it?"

Kristy thought she was tough. But she was not tough enough to walk to school by herself. Kristy and Mary Anne and I walked together—and

Janine walked five steps behind us. She was sort of our babysitter. She hated the job.

Every school morning I would collect my friends. That was *my* job, and I loved it. I always ran across the road to the Thomases' house first. That was where Kristy lived with her mum and dad, her two big brothers, her baby brother David Michael, and their brand new collie puppy Louie. I usually rang the doorbell twice. It was sort of a signal. Then I would stand on the steps and pray that anybody except Mr Thomas would answer the door. I did not like Kristy's father.

Kristy usually answered the door herself, all ready to go. The two of us would run next door to Mary Anne's house, where Mr Spier always answered the door. But that was okay. I liked Mr Spier. He wasn't a lot of fun, but he was nice enough.

"Good morning, Mr Spier!" Kristy and I would say.

"Good morning, girls," he would answer. Then he would turn and call, "Mary Anne! Step along!" (I think that meant hurry up.)

A few moments later, Mary Anne would appear. She would be wearing a dress or a skirt (no jeans allowed) and her hair would be plaited and tied with ribbons. She was never allowed to wear trainers, except on gym days. And even then she had to carry them with her and wear them only during gym (which she could not stand).

74

"Goodbye, Mr Spier!" Kristy and I would say.

"'Bye, Daddy!" Mary Anne would say.

Mr Spier never answered us, exactly. Instead, he stood at the door and called out things like, "Don't get your feet wet!" "Be careful crossing the street!" "Eat your lunch, Mary Anne!"

My friends and I would walk back to my house, and Janine would be there waiting for us. That autumn, Mary Anne and Kristy and I did not have much to carry to school—just our lunches and maybe something for break time. (And three times a week, Mary Anne carried her trainers.) Janine seemed to carry the world around with her. A big bag full of books and papers and science stuff. And she could do one really clever thing. She could walk and read a book at the same time. I was fascinated. I could not even read standing still.

One day in October the four of us set off for school. Janine was reading. I was talking to Kristy. Mary Anne was crying.

"It is *gym* day," she wailed.

"It is also art day," I reminded her. Mary Anne and Kristy liked art class almost as much as I did.

Our art teacher was Miss Packett. She had favourites, and I was not one of these. I think this was because I had trouble paying attention. I didn't care, though. Art class meant I did not have to sit still. I could stand up. I could move around. Best of all, I could use crayons—and other cool things.

"Art day," Mary Anne repeated. "Oh, goody."

Art class was not until the afternoon. The morning seemed long. Mrs Frederickson yelled, I put my hands over my ears, Mary Anne cried, and Kristy got into a fight with Alan Gray in the playground.

But at last, Miss Packett wheeled her art trolley into our room. We spent half an hour finishing our clay sculptures. Then, just before the bell rang, Miss Packett said, "Boys and girls, today I am going to give you . . . art homework."

Homework? We never had homework in first grade. I panicked. I could barely read or write in school. How was I going to do it at home by myself?

But Miss Packett said, "Your homework is to colour a self-portrait. I want each of you to make yours at home because I want you to be able to work on it in peace. I want you to draw yourself in the way you see yourself, not the way your friends see *them*selves. This must be your own work . . . Claudia? Claudia Kishi, are you listening to me?"

I was. Sort of. I was thinking about my self-portrait. I was thinking about my crayons. I was thinking about the wonderful colours I would use.

"Yes," I replied. "I'm listening."

"I hope so." Miss Packett began piling her things back on the art trolley. She always did this loudly. *Smack, smack, smack. Clunk.*

76

Mary Anne raised her hand.

"Yes, Mary Anne?" said Miss Packett.

"Do you want us to draw our—"

"I want you to draw whatever you want to draw," Miss Packett interrupted.

"But with crayons or a pencil or what?" called out Kristy. She never raised her hand. It drove our teachers crazy.

"Whatever you want," Miss Packett repeated crisply. "And *raise* your *hand*, Kristin Thomas ... Kristin?"

"O*kay*." (Kristy was not one of Miss Packett's favourites, either.)

"Please bring your portraits in tomorrow. Give them to Mrs Frederickson. We will look at them on Friday, during our next class."

Miss Packett pushed her trolley out of the room then. I wished that meant school was over, but it did not. We had to struggle through a worksheet first. Every few minutes, Mrs Frederickson would say, "Sit *still*, Claudia," or "Pay *atten*tion, Claudia," or "Eyes on your *pa*per, Claudia."

I did not mind too much. As soon as that paper was filled in I could go home to my crayons. And I would be able to make something beautiful that would please Miss Packett. Maybe it would even please Mrs Frederickson.

When school finally did end, I jumped and skipped and hopped all the way home. "Cool homework," I said to Kristy and Mary Anne.

Claudia

"Easy homework," said Kristy.

"I know exactly what I am going to draw," said Mary Anne.

"Me too," I said. And I did.

8th
CHAPTER

Claudia

I could not wait to start my homework.

"I have homework!" I announced proudly to Mimi when Janine and I came home. (We had walked Mary Anne and Kristy to their houses first.)

"She has *art* homework," said Janine with a scowl.

"Well, it is im*por*—" I started to shout.

"Now, girls," said Mimi gently. "Please." She turned to me. "Tell me about your homework, my Claudia."

"We are going to make self-portraits. We can make them any way we want. With pencils or paints or anything. I am going to crayon mine. I will use every colour."

Janine raised her eyebrows. "What a surprise."

"I bet you could not even draw a *house*," I said to her.

"Why would I want to?"

With Janine, I could never win.

But I was not going to let that bother me. Not when I was about to start a great project. As soon as I had finished my snack, I ran to my room. I pulled out my biggest pad of drawing paper. Then I found the box of sixty-four Crayola crayons with the sharpener.

I sighed with happiness.

And then I began to draw. I started with two wavy lines like this:

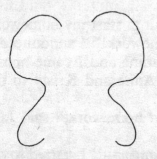

In the middle I added a body. Then I coloured in stripes and splotches and spots. I did not use every crayon in my box, but I used an awful lot of them. The last things I drew were the antennae.

My butterfly—my beautiful, wild, free butterfly—was finished. I had worked on it for almost two hours. It had taken such a long time that I had needed a few breaks. Now I could not wait to show it to Miss Packett. I had finally made something she would admire, even if I did have trouble paying attention.

I rolled up the sheet of paper. Then I slipped three rubber bands over it. That was how Miss Packett had shown us to save our work. We were supposed to carry our portraits carefully to school that way the next day, so they would not get torn or wrinkled.

I put my butterfly on the bench by our front door. I did not want to forget to bring my homework to school. Then I worried that it might roll off and get lost. I kept moving it around the house that evening, until it wound up back on the bench.

The next day, Thursday, I checked on my picture first thing. It was still lying on the bench. I breathed a sigh of relief. I could not wait to deliver it to Mrs Frederickson. Then I could stop worrying about it. If she lost it, it would not be my fault.

That morning Janine walked Kristy and Mary Anne and me to school as usual. My friends and I each carried our rolled-up pictures along with our lunch boxes.

"Let's look at them," said Kristy as we walked along. "I want to show you what I did."

I was horrified. "We cannot unroll them!" I exclaimed. "They will get all wrinkled. Miss Packett would be cross."

81

Mary Anne froze. "Don't anyone open mine then," she said. She held it gingerly away from her.

Kristy grabbed for it.

"Don't!" shrieked Mary Anne.

"Kristy, stop teasing," Janine called from behind us."

"Okay, okay," she said. Then she added, "Bother. I suppose we will have to wait until tomorrow to look at them. I wonder what Alan Gray drew. Probably a gorilla."

Mary Anne and I giggled.

When we reached school, we left our drawings on Mrs Frederickson's desk. A pile of them was already there. We stacked ours on top. Everyone wanted to look at the pictures, but we all knew we would have to wait.

Waiting. Something I was not good at.

But I did wait until Friday afternoon. I had no choice.

When I heard Miss Packett's art trolley roll down the corridor, a shiver ran through me. Soon she would look at my self-portrait. She would probably hold it up for everyone to see. Maybe she would tape it up in the corridor where the whole school could see it.

"Good afternoon, girls and boys," said Miss Packett. "I see you all did your homework." (Mrs

82

Frederickson had just handed her the pile of rolled-up drawings.)

One by one Miss Packett removed the rubber bands, unrolled the portraits, smoothed them out, and held them up.

Mary Anne's was first. She had used markers to colour a picture of a girl with brown plaits and brown eyes. She was smiling and three teeth were missing. "Very nice," said Miss Packett.

Alan Gray's was next. He had not drawn a gorilla. He had drawn a boy with brown hair wearing blue trousers and a red shirt. "Very nice," said Miss Packett again.

Miss Packett held up drawing after drawing. Each one showed a face (sometimes a body, too) with brown or black or blond hair, and brown or black or blue eyes.

I began to have a funny feeling in my stomach.

At last Miss Packett unrolled my drawing. She studied it for a few moments. She frowned. I thought maybe she was not even going to hold it up. But then she did turn it around. And she asked, "Whose drawing is this?"

Oops. I had worked so hard on my picture, and then I had forgotten to put my name on it.

I raised my hand slowly. "It's mine," I said in a small voice.

Nearby, Alan Gray began to snicker.

Then someone giggled.

Soon everyone was giggling.

"Claudia," said Miss Packett sternly, "what is this?"

"My self-portrait," I replied.

"Is this some kind of joke?" Before I could answer, Miss Packett looked around at my laughing classmates. (Well, Mary Anne and Kristy were not laughing, but they looked confused.) "Class! Be quiet!" she ordered. "Claudia, see what you caused? Can't you take anything seriously? I asked for a self-portrait. Like *this*." She reached for one of the other drawings. One of the ones with a squiggle of hair, two eyes, a nose, and a pair of lips.

I could not answer her. If I had, I would have cried. And I was not going to let her see me do that.

I walked home from school that day in disgrace. I hardly said a word, even though Mary Anne and Kristy were being very nice to me. They kept saying what a meanie Miss Packett was.

As soon as I walked through our front door, I burst into tears.

"My Claudia—what is wrong?" Mimi held her arms out to me.

I could not answer.

"Janine? What happened?"

Janine had read all the way home. She did not have a clue.

Finally I calmed down enough to tell Mimi about school.

Mimi's mouth dropped open.

"See? I am just stupid," I said miserably. "I cannot read. I cannot write. I cannot sit still. I did not understand the instructions."

Mimi had set her mouth in a firm line. She stood up. She took my hand in hers. And she said, "Oh, no, my Claudia. That is not true at all. You understood the instructions better than anyone else."

And Mimi marched me out the door and all the way back to school.

"Now where is Miss Packett's classroom?" she asked me as we stepped inside.

"She does not have one," I replied. "Just an office."

We found the office. My timid Mimi stood face-to-face with Miss Packett. I wondered if Mimi would yell. But in the gentlest, most polite voice you can imagine, she said, "Miss Packett, I would like you please to respect my Claudia's intelligence and imagination. She told me what happened in school today, and I believe you are mistaken. Of all of your students, Claudia is the only one who truly understood your assignment. You asked the children to draw themselves the way they see themselves. And my Claudia sees herself as a free spirit, like a butterfly. So that is what she drew."

Mimi turned then and we left.

On Monday, Miss Packett apologized to me. But I did not care about that. What mattered was that Mimi understood what I had done. And that she appreciated and valued my artwork. I spent more and more time drawing and painting. I decided, eventually, that maybe I could become an artist one day. Oh, and I added my name to my butterfly drawing.

I still have the drawing. I looked at it the other day. Written across the bottom is CALUDIA.

Jessi

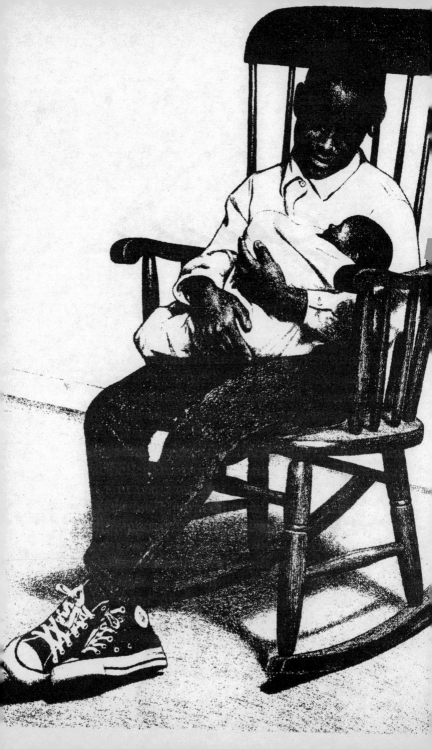

9th CHAPTER

Jessi

Dear Squirt,

Someday when you are big, you will read this letter. Right now you are still little, a toddler. For a little kid, you made an awfully big change in my life. I remember when you were born. (Well, I should. It wasn't that long ago.) But the thing is, I remember it in detail.

I remember it vividly. Do you want to know what your family was like when you were born? Okay, we lived in Oakley, New Jersey then. I was nine years old, almost ten. Becca was six going on seven....

That letter I wrote to my baby brother was not just any letter. For one thing, as you can tell, it was a letter he would probably not read for years. For another, it was not a letter to be posted, or even to be saved in a drawer or a baby book. It was a letter to go in the time capsule Becca and I were making for him.

The time capsule project began one hot summer's day not long after Kristy's slumber party. I was babysitting for Becca and Squirt while Mama and Daddy were at work, and Aunt Cecelia was spending the entire afternoon running errands. Squirt was having a nap and Becca was bored. She often becomes bored in hot weather.

"What can I *do* today?" she whined.

"See if Charlotte can come over," I suggested.

"She can't. She's visiting her aunt."

"Oh. Well, what about someone el—"

"There's no one. Everyone's either at camp or on holiday."

"Then read a book."

"I've just finished one. I want to do something *diff*erent."

"Draw a picture. Build something with lolly sticks."

"No, something *really* different."

Something *really* different. Hmm. That was a challenge. But I hadn't thought long before the idea of the time capsule came to me. Don't ask me where it came from because I don't know. I'm just glad it came. Maybe Kristy's gift for thinking up great ideas is rubbing off on the rest of us. Anyway, I suggested the time capsule to Becca and she was intrigued.

"Gosh, there are so *many* things we could put in it," she said slowly. "A copy of the newspaper so Squirt will know what was going on in the world on this day. And maybe a picture of our family. And let's see, a sample page from the *TV Guide*. . . ."

Becca was off and running. While she searched for the items, I began the letter to Squirt. And before I knew it, my mind had travelled back more than a year and a half to the weeks just before Squirt's birth. I remembered that time as

91

Jessi

clearly as if the events were happening now.

When I was nine years old (well, really almost
ten) I lived with Mama and Daddy and Becca in
our old house in Oakley, New Jersey. I loved that
house. It was the only one I had ever known. It
was not big. In fact, it was on the crowded side
and about to become more crowded. But it was
home. Maybe it didn't feel crowded because back
in Oakley "home" seemed to extend beyond the
doorways of the house. It extended across the
road to where my aunt and uncle and three
cousins lived. It extended next door to my
grandparents' house, and up and down the street
to our neighbours. Most of them had lived in their
houses since long before I had been born. Our
neighbourhood was old and settled and comfortable. People didn't move much. Everybody knew
everybody else (and probably their business, too).
And among those neighbours were more of my
family—other aunts and uncles and cousins.
Keisha, one of the cousins across the street, was
special, though, since at the time she was my best
friend. We had grown up together, just like
Kristy and Mary Anne.

In that neighbourhood, people sat on their
wide front porches on hot summer evenings.
They called on each other. The adults kept
their eyes on the children playing, whether they
were their own or not. In the winter, people

helped each other shovel their cars out from snowdrifts. I could have walked into almost any house on the street and felt comfortable with the family inside.

In June of the year Squirt was born, the summer holiday had just begun. I was a proud graduate of fourth grade. Becca had finished first grade and won an award for reading the most books in her class. I was glad she was a reader. I was looking forward to passing my old books down to her. The end of school was a big event. But not as big as the event which was supposed to take place in four weeks. Mama was going to have another baby. This was a Big Event.

It was big for a couple of reasons. First of all a new baby is always a big event. Especially in our neighbourhood where people liked taking care of one another. Naturally they loved babies. But what made the big event a Big Event was that Mama and Daddy had tried to have another baby after Becca had been born—they'd tried twice— and each time the baby had died before it was born. The first one was a girl, the second one was a boy. This time it seemed that the baby would actually be born, and be born healthy. All kinds of tests had been performed. Mama and Daddy had held their breath as Mama had made it through the third month and then the six month of her pregnancy without problems. Now she was beginning her ninth month. My parents had stopped holding their breath, but they were still very nervous—and excited.

I knew I should be excited, too. But I wasn't. That was my secret. My Big Secret about the Big Event.

I did not want that baby.

A baby would change everything. I remembered what had happened when my friend Morgan got a new baby sister at the beginning of fourth grade. Bang. Nothing was ever the same. Morgan's peaceful life had been interrupted by a noisy, crying, *smelly* little person. No matter what anyone tells you, I thought, babies smell. Milk smells, the stuff they eat smells, and when all the stuff they eat comes out the other end, it *really* smells. The nappy smells, baby powder smells, baby shampoo smells, baby wipes smell, you get the idea.

Almost as bad as the arrival of the noisy, smelly baby was another change that was going to take place in our house. Just before the baby arrived, Becca was going to move into my room. We had always had our own rooms, and I liked it that way. My room was pretty big (considering our house was pretty small), and Becca's was only about half its size, but she didn't seem to care. However, after the baby was born, he or she would get the little room, and Becca and I were going to share the big room. Mama and Daddy said it was sensible, and that was the end of that.

94

I was not happy.

However, I never said a word to anyone about not wanting the baby and not wanting to share a room. How could I? I didn't want to jinx this baby. If I had said I didn't want it and then something had happened to it . . . it was too awful a thought. I pretended to be thrilled that a crying, smelly thing was coming to the house and I would have to give up my privacy. This was why I could not speak up on that fateful Monday morning when the baby began to seem more real and less like just a bad idea.

School had ended on Friday, three days earlier. And—wonder of wonders—Becca and I could sleep late. By the time we rolled out of bed and staggered downstairs for breakfast, Daddy had left for work. And Aunt Cecelia had come over for a cup of coffee. She was sitting in the kitchen with Mama. Becca and I entered the room just in time to hear Mama say, "I will never again be pregnant in the summer. If you ever hear me say something about having an*other* baby, remind me to do it before June."

Mama was in a bad mood because her ankles were swelling.

"Hi, girls," Aunt Cecelia greeted Becca and me.

"Morning," we replied.

Before we had even poured ourselves juice, Mama said, "I have a project for you two. I want to get the baby's room ready, so today, Becca, you'll move into Jessi's room. You can start after breakfast."

I wanted to cry, "To*day*? But the baby isn't due for a month!" I knew better, though. Mama was in a mood.

Unfortunately, Becca had not recognized the mood. "To*day*?" she wailed. (I suppose Becca didn't want to leave her old room any more than I wanted her to invade my room.)

Mama didn't say a word, but she eyed Becca sternly. And I kicked my sister under the table. Then I sent her a Look of my own.

"Okay, Mama," I said. "And while we're at it, maybe Becca and I can clear out some of our old toys for the baby. Then when you and Daddy go shopping, you might not have to buy so much stuff."

Mama and Daddy had not bought a thing for the baby. They still had the old cot and high chair that Becca and I had used. And our car seat and things like that. But they'd given away a lot of our baby clothes. And of course we had none of those smelly baby products. Plus, Becca's room would probably have to be repainted for the baby. And I had heard Mama talk about making new curtains for it. We had a lot to do.

And Becca was ready to complain. As soon as breakfast was over and she and I were upstairs again—and safely out of earshot—she began

96

mumbling to herself. "I don't see why we have to do this *now*. It's practically the first day of the holidays. My friends are going swimming. Anyway, we have a *month*."

"Becca," I said, "cut it out, okay?"

"I don't have any scissors," she said, which was a standard first-grade reply.

I sighed. "Look, I don't like this either, but you know how Mama is. Now come on. Maybe we can go swimming later."

10th CHAPTER

Jessi

Moving our rooms around turned out to be a bigger job than anybody—even Mama and Daddy—had imagined. For one thing, Becca's stuff didn't exactly fit into my room. We jammed her bed in all right. And we were able to stack her bookcase on top of mine. Then we crammed her dresser in behind the door. After that, the door didn't open all the way, and Becca had to close it in order to open her bureau drawers, but we decided we could live with that. However, still left in Becca's room was an armchair (Mama thought she could use it for the baby), a table and two little chairs (Daddy moved them to our basement den), and some lamps and things (we left them for the baby, too).

My room looked like an obstacle course. You

couldn't turn around without tripping over something. Mama said it wouldn't do. Finally, Daddy carried *my* armchair to the living room and a lamp to the den, and we wedged my desk between our beds, saying we could use that as a bedside table. (He gave my bedside table to Keisha.) All these things were done that night, after Becca and I spent the day moving the junk from her wardrobe into mine, and weeding through our toys.

When the move was finished, Mama and Daddy and Becca and I stood looking into what had been Becca's room. The wallpaper suddenly seemed dingy and faded, except for the places where pictures had hung. There it stood out in bright rectangles. The carpet was stained with felt-tips that had rolled off Becca's table while she was colouring. And the curtains were pink and white stripes with a wide lace edge.

"What if the baby is a boy?" said Becca, eyeing the curtains.

"We'll have to do a little decorating, that's all," said Daddy. "I'll buy some paint, and we can strip off the old wallpaper and put up new."

"And I'll make some curtains and have the carpet cleaned," added Mama.

At least the carpet wasn't pink.

"I'm glad this baby is still four weeks off," said Daddy.

99

So was I. That meant four weeks before the stinky nappies and things moved in.

By the following Saturday, the baby's room looked like, well, it looked like just what it was—a big fat mess. Daddy was about to start stripping off the wallpaper. Dustsheets covered the floor, which was bare, since the carpet was out being cleaned. Paint pots and brushes were stacked in a corner. Tools were in another corner, and some cleaning supplies were in a third. And Mama had been sanding something, so plaster dust was everywhere.

At breakfast, Daddy started listing the things he hoped to accomplish that day. Then Mama added to the list. She wanted to go to Price Busters and stock up on nappies, vests, sleepsuits, lotion, wipes, shampoo, and other baby things. She was making her list when she stopped talking and put her hand over the bulge in her middle. Her eyes opened wide.

"Honey? What is it?" Daddy was at her side in a flash. "Is something wrong?" I knew he was thinking about the two other babies. He looked terrified.

"Not exactly *wrong*," said Mama, gasping a little. "I think the baby is coming." She sounded apologetic.

"Are you sure?" asked Daddy.

Mama gasped again, then gritted her teeth. "Positive."

I have never seen things happen so fast. Daddy started giving orders like an army general. "Jessi, go upstairs and pack a bag for your mother."

Pack a *bag* for her? For a grown-up woman? A grown-up *pregnant* woman? What was I supposed to pack? Bras? If so, how many? And how much of that big underwear?

Mama saw the panic on my face, and said, "I can pack the bag, dear. I have enough time . . . I think."

"All right," said Daddy. "Then Becca, you help your mother. Jessi, you clean up the kitchen. I'll call Aunt Cecelia."

Long ago, Mama and Daddy and Aunt Cecelia had decided that when the baby was born and Mama was in the hospital, Aunt Cecelia would come to the house and stay with Becca and me. Of course, we had thought that would be in the middle of July, so that was when Aunt Cecelia had said she'd "go on standby." Now, she didn't answer Daddy's phone call.

"Run across the street and see if you and Becca can go to Keisha's for a while," Daddy started to say before he remembered that Keisha and her family were leaving to go on holiday that morning. And my grandparents were going with them. Sure enough, I looked out the window just in time to see their loaded-down car pull out of the drive. So Daddy called Mrs Jasper who lived by herself in the house on the other side of ours, and she hustled over. She said she could stay all day if necessary.

During the next twenty minutes, Daddy accomplished about a zillion things. He helped Mama with her suitcase. He told me to keep calling Aunt Cecelia until I reached her, and to ask her to come over as soon as possible and relieve Mrs Jasper. He wrote down a few instructions and some phone numbers for Mrs Jasper. Then he jotted down Mama's entire Price Busters list (how he remembered it, I'll never know) and said to give it to Aunt Cecelia. "See if you three can go shopping there tomorrow—it should be open on Sunday—and tell Aunt Cecelia I'll pay her back as soon as I can."

"Daddy? What about the baby's room?" I asked.

"Show it to Aunt Cecelia. She'll work out something." What, I wasn't sure. I didn't see what Aunt Cecelia could possibly do about that room unless she was a wizard. But I promised Daddy I'd show it to her.

Then he and Mama left in a hurry.

Becca and I found ourselves standing in the kitchen with Mrs Jasper, who was not our favourite person in the world. This and the day's sudden confusion added to my feelings about the baby. On top of everything else, I reckoned that only forty-eight hours or so stood between me and the stinky nappies.

102

I reached Aunt Cecelia just before midday. Becca and Mrs Jasper were sitting in the dim living room (Mrs Jasper had pulled down every blind in our house to prevent it from becoming too hot), playing their zillionth game of Junior Scrabble. What Becca really wanted to do was run outside and play in the sunlight, but Mrs Jasper said she could keep a better eye on us if we didn't leave the house.

So I was relieved to hear that Aunt Cecelia could come over around two o'clock, prepared to stay until whenever Mama and the baby left the hospital. Aunt Cecelia might have been strict, but at least we knew what we were getting into with her.

By two-thirty, the babysitter switch had taken place. Mrs Jasper had left, and Aunt Cecelia and her suitcase and a bag of groceries had arrived. (Aunt Cecelia believes in the importance of vegetables.) Boy, did Aunt Cecelia keep Becca and me hopping. We drove to Price Busters that very afternoon and bought every single item on Daddy's list. Then we came home and Aunt Cecelia started cooking up a storm. When she reached a good stopping place, she took a look in the baby's room. She didn't perform any wizardry, but she did solve our problem. "The baby can sleep in your parents' room for a while," she announced. "I'll finish the curtains to-morrow, and ask the cleaner to return the rug as

103

soon as possible. Then after your father strips off the wallpaper, maybe he can just paint the room. That might be quicker than putting up new paper. The room will be ready before you know it."

The last thing Daddy had called to Becca and me that morning as he and Mama had hurried out the door was, "I'll phone whenever we have news!"

He had not phoned by the time Mrs Jasper left. He had not phoned by the time Aunt Cecelia and Becca and I returned from Price Busters (or if he had, he hadn't left a message on the machine). And he hadn't phoned during Aunt Cecelia's cooking frenzy. But as we stood surveying the baby's room, the telephone rang. The three of us nearly trampled each other in our dash to the kitchen, and I snatched up the receiver first.

"Hello?" I said breathlessly.

"Hi, sweetheart," said Daddy's voice. "You're a big sister again."

"I am?"

"Yup. You and Becca have a little brother, John Philip Ramsey, Junior. He's tiny, but he's fine. He and Mama will be home on Monday."

Daddy gave this news to Becca, and then he spoke to Aunt Cecelia. Aunt Cecelia asked all sorts of questions about the birth and the delivery, although she didn't always seem pleased with the answers Daddy gave her. When he said he had cut the baby's umbilical cord himself, she made a face. (*I* thought that was pretty cool.)

When Aunt Cecelia finally hung up the phone, she said, "Guess what. You two can see your brother tonight."

I tried to feel excited. I really did. But I just could not. I pretended to be excited for Becca's sake, though. Becca looked scared and nervous.

Aunt Cecelia drove us to the hospital after supper. All the way there I kept saying things to Becca such as, "We can pretend the baby is our doll. We can dress him and hold him and take him for walks in the pram." Or, "You'll see how much fun a baby can be." Or, "Now *you* can be a big sister, too."

When we arrived at the hospital, Aunt Cecelia led Becca and me inside, saying how lucky we were to be able to see the baby in the hospital. Not all hospitals allowed children to do that. She reminded us six times to behave.

Ten minutes later, Becca and I were standing with Daddy and Aunt Cecelia in front of a window. Behind it was a roomful of babies. Daddy pointed out Squirt, and my stomach flip-flopped. He was the tiniest, ugliest baby I had ever seen. And he was crying his head off.

11th CHAPTER

Jessi

On the way home from the hospital, Becca nudged me in the ribs and whispered, "I do not want *that* to come and live with us."

I knew she meant the baby. "Neither do I," I whispered back.

"And I hate his name."

"Me too." Who ever heard of a baby named Squirt? That was what the nurses had started calling him because he was the smallest baby in the hospital, since he had been born early. My parents thought it was cute. Becca and I thought it was stupid. "I will never call him Squirt," I said.

"What are you two whispering about back there?" Aunt Cecelia asked.

106

"Nothing," Becca and I replied.

On Sunday, Aunt Cecelia kept us busy again. She said she wanted Mama to come home to a clean house and a full refrigerator on Monday, so she and Daddy wouldn't have to worry about those things and could concentrate on Squirt instead. We cooked and cleaned and set up some baby things in Mama and Daddy's room. Aunt Cecelia finished the curtains. Daddy spent the morning at the hospital, but then came home and worked on the baby's room for hours. He thought he could finish it in a week if he took a little time off from his job, which he'd been planning to do anyway.

On Monday morning, Aunt Cecelia woke Becca and me by standing in the doorway of our room and announcing, "It's baby brother day!"

"Oh, goody," I mumbled.

There was one good thing about Monday, though. It meant Sunday was over. And that meant the cooking and cleaning were over. On the other hand, John Philip Ramsey, Junior, was about to show up.

Mama and Daddy pulled into our drive just after eleven o'clock that morning. The entire neighbourhood was waiting for them. Some people were in our garden. Most of the rest of them were standing on their porches waving at the car as Daddy steered it along. Our street

107

looked like a parade with just one car in it.

"Congratulations!" people called softly.

Mama and Daddy grinned. They made their way to our front garden. At that point, Becca and I couldn't contain ourselves any longer. We might not have been crazy about the baby, but we really had missed Mama. We flew along the path and threw ourselves at her. She handed John Philip to Daddy just in time. Then the three of us hugged and hugged. Mama cried a little. "I *missed* you," she said. "Oh, I am so glad to be home."

We straightened up. We walked inside. Daddy followed us with John Philip. (Becca had said she was going to call the baby It, but I couldn't bring myself to do that. I just planned to call him by his real name. If Mama and Daddy wanted to call him Squirt that was their business.)

The afternoon passed. It was not as smelly as I'd thought it would be. I had to admit that. But it was noisy. No, it was Noisy. In fact, it was NOISY. Becca actually went to Mrs Jasper's to escape. And when Mrs Jasper invited her to dinner, she stayed, even though it was steamed cauliflower night.

John Philip Ramsey, Junior, was a crier.

Anybody who knows me now would probably never guess that Squirt and I got off to such a bad start. But we did. Neither Becca nor I wanted a baby in the first place. Then after he arrived, well, let me say just one word: colic. It's a dreaded word. Ask any parent. However, that dreaded word was what, eventually, brought Squirt and me together.

Okay, back to that afternoon. Squirt cried for hours. Mrs Jasper and Becca could hear him next door. The neighbour across the street called to ask if Mama needed any help. Around three-thirty I retreated to my room, put on my Walkman, and cranked up the volume (I would have joined Becca at Mrs Jasper's, but I could already smell the cauliflower).

Downstairs, Mama and Daddy and Aunt Cecelia (who was staying for a few days to help out) hovered around the baby. Every so often I would take off my earphones to see if the crying had stopped, and I would hear snatches of their conversation.

Once I heard Mama say, "He did cry a lot in the hospital. I don't remember Jessi or Becca crying so much." (I thought of his scrunched-up face as he had cried through our visit to the nursery.)

Another time I heard Aunt Cecelia say disapprovingly, "It isn't natural." I could picture her pursed lips.

And another time I heard that word. Colic. Daddy said it with such fear that I turned off the Walkman and made a beeline for the old baby

109

care book that Daddy had unearthed the week before.

Colic. I didn't even know how to spell it. I looked under K first, then C. Somehow I mixed up "colic" and "cauliflower" and tried to find it under CAU before I finally looked up COLIC. I turned to the first page listed. I nearly fainted. I found myself reading about infants who might cry for hours on end, infants who could not be consoled. And the cause of colic was very bad stomach-aches (as far as I could tell), which even doctors don't really know the cause of.

I swallowed hard. The next sentence on the page screamed out at me. "Colic usually disappears by the third month." I think the author of the book had meant this to be reassuring. But all I could think was: three more months of *this*? I'd barely been able to stand the first four hours. Becca would probably ask to be adopted by Mrs Jasper. Maybe she would even learn to like cauliflower.

I tried to console myself with the thought that John Philip was just having a bad day. He'd been disrupted by the move from the hospital to our house. But that wasn't it at all. By Friday, Mama had taken him to the doctor twice. The result? John Philip was a colicky baby.

And he cried most of the time.

We were all exhausted. But no one was more

exhausted than Mama. Daddy had had to go back to work on Thursday. Aunt Cecelia was still around, but I noticed she left the house pretty often to run errands, and anyway only Mama could feed John Philip. (Mama did not believe in bottle feeding.) So that is how it happened that on a sticky June afternoon when the baby started to cry for the nine billionth time that day, I was the only one to hear him. Daddy was at his office. Aunt Cecelia had taken Becca grocery shopping. And Mama was so tired she'd fallen fast asleep.

"Wahhhh!"

John Philip was in his cot in Mama and Daddy's room. Mama was lying on the couch in the living room. I was in my own room, my headphones practically glued to my ears.

I heard those cries anyway. I waited for Mama to get up. But the cries continued. That was when I peeped downstairs and saw Mama fast asleep. I knew what I had to do.

Timidly, I approached John Philip in his cot.

"Hey. Hey there, John Philip."

"Wahhhh!"

"Well, I know your stomach hurts," I said, as John Philip wailed away, pulling his knees up tightly to his chest.

"Wahhhh!"

I couldn't just let him lie there and scream. So I reached into the cot and picked up the baby the way Mama had shown me, supporting his head

111

with one of my hands. Then I sat down in a rocking-chair, cradling him, and sang him some songs from *Annie*. He especially liked "Tomorrow," and before I knew it, his cries were fading away.

I reached the end of the song. While I was trying to decide on the next one, John Philip started up again, so I started "Tomorrow" again.

His cries stopped.

I knew better than to stop singing, though. "Bet your bottom dollar that tomorrow, there'll be sun," I sang. I looked down at my baby brother. He really was just a little squirt. Maybe the nurses hadn't had such a bad idea. Squirt was a cute nickname.

I leaned over and sniffed my brother. He didn't smell too bad, either. Kind of powdery and milky. Not my choice for a perfume, but I could live with it. He definitely wasn't stinky.

Squirt and I sang and rocked and rocked and sang. At some point, I glanced up and saw Mama leaning against the doorway. She was just standing there, smiling at Squirt and me. She waited for me to reach the end of a verse of "Tomorrow." Then she said, "You're the only one who can calm him down, Jessi."

And for a while—for the next month or so—that was true. So I spent an awful lot of time with Squirt. When he finally got over his colic, I felt as if he'd been with me all my life. I couldn't imagine ever not wanting him, or calling him John Philip Ramsey, Junior, or It, or worrying about his nappies. He was my own little brother, my Squirt. And that moment when I first stopped his wails was my most vivid memory.

LOGAN

12th CHAPTER

LOGAN

WEDNESDAY NIGHT

DEAR MARY ANNE,

IT IS VERY LATE. I AM WRITING
THIS TO YOU AFTER EVERYONE IN
MY FAMILY HAS GONE TO SLEEP
AND OUR HOUSE IS FINALLY QUIET.
I KNOW YOU SAVE LETTERS AND
NOTES AND SENTIMENTAL THINGS
IN THAT CEDAR BOX YOUR GRAND-
MOTHER GAVE YOU, SO HERE'S
SOMETHING ELSE YOU CAN STICK
IN IT. (I MEAN, IF YOU WANT TO.)
REMEMBER WHEN YOU TOLD ME
ABOUT THAT GAME YOU GUYS PLAYED
AT KRISTY'S? ABOUT TRYING TO
DECIDE ON YOUR MOST VIVID

MEMORY? WELL, I DIDN'T HAVE TO
THINK LONG TO COME UP WITH MINE.
AND SINCE IT'S ABOUT YOU, I
THOUGHT I'D WRITE IT DOWN AND
SEND IT TO YOU . . . .

My memory is from about a year ago. It starts with the time my family and I were moving from Louisville, Kentucky, to Stoneybrook, Connecticut. This was not a good period in my life. Why? Because I did not want to move. Louisville was my home. I didn't see how I could be happy anywhere else. Furthermore, I didn't see why we had to *drive* from Kentucky to Connecticut. Why couldn't we *fly* to our new home like normal people? But Dad kept saying the road trip would be educational. He wanted to show the country to Hunter and Kerry and me. (By the way, at the time, Hunter had recently had his birthday, so he had just turned five, and Kerry was about to turn ten.)

"Why do we have to see the country now? Right in the middle of this trauma in our lives?" I asked Dad. "Can't we just get to the new place, adjust to it, and see the country when we are sane?"

"Logan. We are perfectly sane right now." (I

was trying my father's patience.) "Besides, I think the trip will be a nice transition between the old and the new." Dad paused. "You can start a bumper sticker collection or something."

This was not a good trade-off. A bumper sticker collection for my life.

My father had mapped out this roundabout route that would take my family and me north to Ohio, southeast to West Virginia, then northeast through Pennsylvania and New York, and finally east to Connecticut. I reckoned with another couple of blips on the route we could hit New Jersey and Maryland, too, but I didn't want to prolong the trip. Five states in five days was more than enough, especially when no one would really be able to concentrate on the trip anyway. Our minds would be ahead in Connecticut and our hearts would be behind in Kentucky. Where would our stuff be? With any luck, it would be waiting for us—a huge vanful—in Stoneybrook when we arrived.

Our trip started off okay, once Mum finished saying goodbye to the neighbours and crying. In the car Kerry and Hunter were occupied with an enormous stack of new colouring books, sticker books, comic books, and activity books. I read. Mum knitted. Dad drove, choosing back roads and reading aloud the signs about historic sights.

That was on Saturday. By Thursday, when we crossed the border into Connecticut, the scenario

119

was a little different. Mum was driving, Hunter and Kerry were fighting, Dad was the referee, and I was colouring a picture called "Baby Animals on the Farm" in one of Hunter's books. I had just finished "Our Feathered Friends."

Finally Dad decided he had had enough of the fighting. "Stop the car, dear," he said politely to Mum. The moment the car stopped, the fighting stopped. Hunter and Kerry knew Dad had reached the end of his tether. "Time to swap places," announced Dad. He stepped out of the car, opened one front door and one back door, hauled my brother and sister out of the back seat, put Kerry in the front with Mum, put Hunter in the back with the suitcases, then slid in next to me. "Okay, drive on!" he called.

Hunter and Kerry were silent. I finished "Baby Animals on the Farm." Mum stopped for petrol. After she had paid the attendant I said to Dad, "Everyone here talks with accents."

"They'll say the same thing about us," he replied.

Great. Something else to worry about. I was already pretty sure I wouldn't fit in at my new school.

Hunter couldn't have cared less. Actually, I think he was looking forward to the move. "I will have a dew roob," he said. (Hunter is allergic to everything important in life and almost always has a stuffed-up nose.) "Add I will get to start kiddergarted. Hey, baby sub fud kids will live dex door!" (In case you didn't get the last part, Hunter had tried to say, "Hey, maybe some fun kids will live next door!") He beamed at me from where he sat squashed between a suitcase and the picnic basket.

I wasn't sure how Kerry felt about the move. She hadn't said much. But she didn't seem brokenhearted or anything.

"Look!" exclaimed Mum from the driver's seat. "Stoneybrook—twenty kilometres. We're almost there."

"Goody," I muttered.

"What was that?" asked Dad.

"Nothing. Hunter? Can I colour—"

"No!" he replied. "You're going to use up the book." He grabbed it away.

I stared out the window as we drove closer and closer to Doom.

Mum and Dad had a little trouble finding the house. When we finally pulled into the drive I saw, to tell the honest truth, a house that didn't look *too* different from the one we'd left behind. An average house on an average street with a nice little garden. And a removal van parked in front. I was awfully relieved to see that van. My football and a lot of other important things were in it, and my cousin had told me these horror stories about bogus removal vans driving off full of entire households and never showing up again.

Mum and Dad began talking to the removal men, and I eased myself out of the car. My knees creaked from having been bent into the same position for five days. I looked up and down the street. It was quiet, not a person in sight. Everyone was probably away on summer holidays. I imagined them at camp sites and museums and amusement parks, speaking with their East Coast accents.

School was supposed to begin on Thursday of the following week, after Labour Day. I had exactly one week to adjust to my new life before entering the doorway of Stoneybrook Middle School. Why, I thought, couldn't we at least have moved a year later, when I'd be starting high school? Then all the ninth-graders would be new to school. In eighth grade I'd stick out like a sore thumb, unless there was a whole fleet of us new kids, which I doubted.

Mum and Dad tried hard to help Hunter and Kerry and me adjust to Stoneybrook. They drove us around so we could see where the cinema and the supermarket and our schools were. (All Hunter wanted to know was whether Stoneybrook had a dump. He likes junk.) They walked us through town so we could see the shops. They invited the neighbours over. They tried to unpack quickly so the house would feel like a home, even if it wasn't our old house.

On Wednesday night, the night before school

began, I stood in front of the bathroom mirror. I decided my hair and my teeth looked strange. I had a spot on my chin. I was pretty sure my clothes were all wrong. And what if the boys at SMS didn't like football?

It was 8.21 a.m. on Thursday morning. I was standing near the front doors of SMS. Kids were streaming by me, talking a mile a minute. Finally I joined them. No one said a word to me. I'm not sure anyone even noticed me. (Hey, maybe I was invisible!) Was this good or bad? It could have meant I looked fine and fitted in so well that no one could tell I was new. Or it could have meant the kids were snobs and were ignoring me.

I flattened myself against a wall, away from the shouting kids, and studied my timetable. My classroom was 212. Okay. Second floor. Now where were the stairs?

I stepped into the crowd, hesitated, and was nearly run over.

"Hey! Move it!" someone yelled.

"Okay, okay."

Someone grabbed my elbow, a guy my age. "You lost?" he asked.

"Who me? Of course not."

The guy frowned. "Where are you from?"

I almost said, "Mars." Then I thought better of it. "Louisville." I hurried on as if I knew exactly where I was going.

123

Somehow I made it through the morning and even wound up in the cafeteria at lunchtime. I had to admit that the morning had not been quite as bad as I'd thought it would be. In my classroom this very nice girl named Stacey or maybe Tracey (I couldn't remember which it was) had introduced herself to me. When I told her where I was from she had just nodded. But she'd turned up in my English class later, and had remembered my name (even if I hadn't remembered hers).

Now I gazed around the cafeteria wondering where to sit. I got prepared to sit by myself and feel dorky. And alone.

13th
CHAPTER

LOGAN

I had refused to let Mum or Dad pack a lunch for me, even though our refrigerator was full of great food from the neighbours. I didn't know whether kids at SMS brought packed lunches. In case that was a very nerdy thing to do, I opted to bring money with me and buy lunch at school, no matter how bad the food was.

Now I was sitting (by myself) behind a tray containing a plate covered with noodles buried under mushrooms and cream sauce. I knew that's what the gooey grey mess was because I had read the menu stuck near the start of the queue. It's a good thing that menu was there. It certainly helped in identifying the items on my plate.

I sat with my fork poised above the noodles. I

125

thought about the pickles and cold meat in the refrigerator at home.

I lowered the fork. I raised it again. I couldn't quite . . .

And then I glanced across the cafeteria. I don't know why. My attention was simply drawn there, drawn to this table full of girls. One of them was Stacey-or-Tracey. But she wasn't what had drawn my attention. I was looking at the girl sitting next to her.

And she was looking at me.

Strangely, she looked as if she'd seen a ghost. What was wrong with me? I glanced down at my clothes. They seemed all right. At any rate, my shirt wasn't on backwards, and I couldn't have spilled anything on myself because I hadn't managed to take a bite of those noodle things yet.

The girl turned to Stacey-or-Tracey then and whispered something to her. I looked away. And a hand clapped down on my shoulder.

"Hey," said a guy's voice. "You're the new kid, right?"

I nodded. (Was I really the *only* new kid?)

"I'm Pete Black. And this is Rick Chow and Alan Gray and Trevor Sandbourne. And you're kind of sitting at our table."

These four guys were climbing over the backs of the chairs, holding trays, and settling themselves around me.

"I am?" I replied. "I didn't—I mean, no one

126

was here." I started to stand up. "I'll just move—"

"No, that's okay. You can stay here," said one of them. (I had no idea who was who.) "You looked sort of—"

"Dorky?" I suggested.

The guys laughed. Then they began to concentrate on opening their milk cartons. Finally, they did what I'd done a few moments earlier. They sat with their forks poised above the food, if you could call it that.

"Gross," one of them said. But then he found the nerve to put a forkful of the stuff in his mouth. "Could be worse," he said, and we all dug in. I suppose it *could* have been worse, but I wasn't sure how.

By the time lunch was over, horrible as it had been, I felt better. The guys had been okay, really friendly, and I hadn't sat alone after all.

In the corridor we split up—after Rick pointed me in the direction of my next class. I walked confidently through the crowded corridors. I had been late to every one of my classes that morning because I'd had trouble finding them. At least now I wouldn't be late.

As I rounded the corner to the corridor where Rick had promised my classroom would be, I saw her again. The girl from the cafeteria. She was walking towards me with two of the other girls she'd been sitting with, but not Stacey-or-Tracey.

This time she didn't see me. She and her friends were talking and laughing, and I could tell they were going to walk right by me. So I took this as an opportunity to slow down and look at her.

The truth is, she wasn't glamorous or sophisticated or . . . or a lot of other things. She was pretty, but that wasn't why I was looking at her. I had no idea why I was so drawn to her. But I knew that for ever after I'd be able to tell anyone who asked just what she was wearing that day. And it wasn't glamorous or sophisticated either, not a bit like the wild outfit Stacey-or-Tracey had been wearing. She was wearing a simple dress over a white T-shirt with kneesocks and loafers. Her brown hair was combed loose over her shoulders. She wasn't wearing any jewellery.

But she was special. I just knew it.

One second later she and her friends had passed by. I stood gawping after them. I stood for so long that the bell rang and I was late to my next class after all. But I didn't care. The only thing that mattered in my life just then was seeing that girl again, and maybe finding out her name.

That afternoon I spotted her crossing the car-park after school. I saw her in the hallway the next morning. And I saw her in the cafeteria at lunchtime.

Okay, I had seen her again.

128

The next step was to find out her name. I was eating lunch with Rick and Alan and the other guys. I knew I could ask them who she was and they'd probably know. I also knew they'd give me a hard time.

So I tried other methods.

First I followed her. And I didn't wait long to do it. I followed her right out of the cafeteria that day. She headed right for the girls' cloakroom. I couldn't follow her in *there*. And I was too embarrassed to wait around outside for her. So I let her go.

The second time I followed her she just went into a classroom. This wasn't getting me anywhere. Finally I screwed up my courage and at lunchtime on Monday I asked Pete Black who she was. Pete cuffed my ear, Alan whacked me on the back, and Rick poked me in the ribs. "Go, Logan!" said Trevor.

Once all that was out of their systems they gave me plenty of information. Her name was Mary Anne Spier. The friends she was sitting with were Dawn Schafer, Claudia Kishi, Stacey McGill (oh, *Sta*cey), and Kristy Thomas. She was really nice but *really* shy. She did not have (and never had had) a boyfriend.

Good. This was a good start. But I needed more.

"What else do you know about her?" I asked.

"She hates sports," said Alan, "and she likes to babysit."

Great. A little more detective work and I'd found out that a) those girls ran a business called the Babysitters Club, and b) their club was in trouble. They were being offered more jobs than they could manage and needed extra sitters to cover for them. They only wanted experienced sitters, though.

An idea was beginning to take shape.

I didn't do anything with it until several days later. I had become a pretty good spy by then and had found out that the girls were going to hold what they called "an emergency meeting of the BSC" at lunchtime. So I convinced Pete and the guys to move to the other end of the long table at which the girls were sitting. Then, from down the table, I watched the girls until I was pretty sure they were actually holding the meeting. I approached them—just in time to hear Claudia Kishi say that they better find some way to solve the problem, which was that they were too busy.

That was when I spoke up. I said, "I've done a lot of babysitting." (That was true. And not just for Hunter and Kerry.) The girls were looking at me in surprise, so I added, "In Louisville. I've had plenty of experience."

"*Really?*" asked Stacey.

They began talking at once, all except Mary

Anne. (I was glad I'd been warned that she was shy.)

The next thing I knew I was sitting with them—next to Mary Anne, of course—and Pete and the guys were calling encouraging things to me from their seats. Then Kristy began telling me about the Babysitters Club, and I told her about my sitting experiences and how late I could stay out and stuff. And the *next* thing I knew, Kristy had invited me to a club meeting.

That was how, on a weekday afternoon at a few minutes before five-thirty, I came to be standing on Claudia Kishi's doorstep, ringing her bell. A few moments later she answered it. And led me upstairs to . . . her bedroom.

I had not expected that. I'd envisioned us sitting around a kitchen table, or maybe even outdoors on patio furniture. But not in her bedroom. The other girls were there already. "Hey, everybody," I greeted them from Claudia's doorway. I saw an empty space on the floor next to Mary Anne, so I sat in it before Claudia could. Then because I thought maybe I'd seemed too eager, I said, "Mary Anne, right?" as I settled down.

She just nodded. Didn't she *ever* speak?

"So. What do we do here?" I asked finally.

And again they all started talking at once— except for Mary Anne.

During that meeting the phone rang a lot and I

131

watched the girls line up babysitting jobs. There were a few embarrassing moments (like when Claudia almost said *bra strap* in front of me, and when I started to tell this story I realized I couldn't finish with an audience of girls) but mostly it was okay. Except that Mary Anne just did not *talk*.

Finally at the end of the meeting this great thing happened, though. A job was offered to the club and Kristy wanted me to take it—along with one of the club members so someone could make sure I really was a safe and decent sitter. The job was for this family, new clients named Rodowsky, and the only person who was free to go with me was Mary Anne. "I think we've got the job," I said to her.

She looked ready to keel over. "I think so," she replied in a whisper.

14th CHAPTER

LOGAN

Mary Anne and I were supposed to be at the Rodowskys' the following Thursday from three-thirty until six. Mary Anne said to meet her there a little early. It was one of the few things she had said to me since the meeting the week before. That was okay with me. I don't mind quiet people.

On Thursday, I had just enough time to run home after school, change my shirt, and slap on some of Dad's after-shave. Then I ran over to Reilly Lane, found the Rodowskys' house, and saw Mary Anne crossing the street towards it at the same time.

"Hi!" I called.

"Hi!" replied Mary Anne. She actually smiled. (And what a great smile she had. Her whole face smiled.)

133

"Ready?" I asked her.

"I hope so. How much trouble can one kid be?"

Mary Anne and I walked to the front door and I rang the bell. A lady let us inside. Then she called, "Jackie! Your sitters are here." A moment later this redheaded kid tore into the hallway, almost running into Mary Anne.

"This is Jackie," said his mother, introducing Mary Anne and me to him.

Some kids freak out with new sitters, but not Jackie. He just said, "I've got a grasshopper. Wanna see him?"

Mrs Rodowsky needed to talk to Mary Anne and me for a few minutes, though. She had to tell us where she could be reached and stuff like that. Then she left, with two other little redheaded boys in tow.

"They're my brothers," Jackie informed Mary Anne and me. "Their names are Shea and Archie. Shea's nine and Archie's four. They get to take lessons at the gym."

"Don't you take lessons?" Mary Anne asked him.

"Nope. On account of I'm a handful," replied Jackie matter-of-factly.

I glanced at Mary Anne. A handful? A kind of Dennis the Menace maybe? I began to wonder what I'd got myself into. I knew Mary Anne was going to be watching me to see how I handled things. And I wanted the job to go perfectly. No accidents, no spills, nothing.

I decided to think of something quiet to engage Jackie in, and I was about to ask him if he wanted to play draughts, when Jackie leaped on to the couch in the playroom. "Boing, boing, boing!" he cried as he jumped up and down. "I'm a basketball! Watch me make a basket!"

Jackie hurled himself off the couch and through the air. I caught him before he crashed into the piano.

Mary Anne looked impressed (or maybe just relieved), which I took as a good sign. However, this job was not going the way I'd hoped. I decided to act as if I'd seen a million little kids fly through the air and nearly cream themselves on pianos though.

With Jackie still in my arms I raised him above my head and shouted, "Yes, it's the deciding basket, fans!" I pretended Jackie was a human basketball. Then I got him away from the couch as fast as I could.

It worked. Jackie was laughing. He said he wanted to show Mary Anne and me his grasshopper. "His name is Elizabeth," Jackie added.

"You've got a grasshopper named Elizabeth?" I repeated.

"A *boy* grasshopper?" added Mary Anne.

"Yup. Be right back."

Jackie made a dash for the stairs.

"Whoa. That kid's got energy," I said to Mary Anne.

She just nodded. I headed for the living room to wait for Jackie. I wandered around, looking at the paintings on the walls. Why was Mary Anne so quiet? I was beginning to wonder how I was going to get to know someone so quiet. I couldn't keep up one-sided conversations for ever. Eventually, I would run out of stuff to say.

Surprisingly, Mary Anne finally did say something, and on her own, too. She checked her watch, then stammered, "It's, um, it's—it's taking Jackie an awfully long time to—"

CRASH!

A horrible sound came from upstairs, and it was followed by a cry. I knew exactly what the rest of Mary Anne's sentence would have been. "—get the grasshopper." In other words, why wasn't I checking on him?

Well, I should have checked on him, but I hadn't, and now it was too late. Jackie had had some sort of accident. I hoped it wasn't a bad one. But so what? I had let an accident (bad or not) happen. I could almost *see* Mary Anne thinking, Stee-rike one!

I took the stairs two at a time. Mary Anne was right behind me.

"Jackie! Where are you?" I shouted.

"Ow!" he replied. "I'm in the bathroom."

The Rodowskys' house seemed to be laid out

exactly like our new house. The same person must have built them. So I had a pretty good idea where the bathroom was. I turned left.

And there was Jackie. He was sitting on the bathroom floor in the middle of the shower curtain. Behind him, the shower rod was sticking out of the bathtub. I had a feeling I knew what had happened, but first things first. "Are you hurt?" I asked. I sat down next to him.

"Nope."

"Well, what happened?"

"Okay, see, today in gym we were exercising. We were climbing ropes and swinging on these bars—"

I knew it! "And you thought you'd try swinging on the curtain rod," I supplied. (Mary Anne looked shocked, as if I were a mind reader.)

Actually, Jackie looked a little surprised himself. "Yeah," he said. "How did you know?"

"I did it myself once."

Jackie let out a deep breath. He looked fascinated as I told him that after *my* accident, I needed six stitches in my lip.

At this point, Mary Anne interrupted our boys' talk, saying we ought to check Jackie over, even though he had said he wasn't hurt.

Uh-oh. Of course I should have done that, and I should have done it right away. Stee-rike two.

Mary Anne got to work, checking for bruises

137

and bumps. She found one bruise on Jackie's knee, but otherwise he seemed okay.

"Sorry," I said to Mary Anne. "I'm glad you're here."

Mary Anne grinned. She didn't look angry, or even annoyed. So I decided to play a little game I have invented for times when things aren't going so well. It's called Clean Slate. In this game, you mentally give yourself another chance. You get to start all over again. In other words, you wipe the slate clean. Okay, I was going to forget about the human cannonball, and letting Dennis the Menace go upstairs by himself, and then not checking him for injuries after his accident.

You *are* a good sitter, I told myself. You know it. And starting from now you are going to act like it. I even erased my two stee-rikes and pretended the scoreboard was as clean as the slate.

"I need some juice," Jackie announced, as he and Mary Anne and I headed downstairs. He ran for the kitchen.

Juice. Now that was something I could handle. When Jackie emerged from the fridge with a bottle of grape juice, I said, with great assurance, "Better let me pour."

"No, no. I can do it," said Jackie.

I was torn. Should I risk a spill? Or should I let Jackie show off his independence? After all, I wouldn't want to inhibit him.

Before I could make up my mind, Jackie had

138

filled a paper cup with juice. And he had not spilled a drop. Which was why I thought letting him carry the cup out of the kitchen would be okay.

As soon as I heard Jackie say, "Oops," I knew I had been wrong. Stee-rike one. However, after I had got most of the stain out of the living room carpet (which luckily was dark blue) using soda water and a few other things, I took back the stee-rike. Mary Anne looked impressed again. And later, after Jackie had got his hand stuck in Elizabeth's jar and I had freed him using margarine, Mary Anne looked positively pleased.

"Good thinking!" she said.

By then, I had lost all track of where I might be, stee-rike wise. I decided to wait until the end of the sitting job to find out. The end, by the way, came after Jackie had fallen off his bicycle, ripped his jeans, and accidentally tripped Mary Anne, causing her to stumble backwards. I caught her. In my arms.

When Mary Anne and I finally escaped from the Rodowskys' house, her silence seemed to have been broken. "You were great," she said, the moment the door closed behind us. "Really great."

"Are you kidding me? After all those accidents?"

"Jackie's accident-prone," replied Mary Anne. "That's all. It's too bad he thinks he's a handful,

139

because he doesn't do those things on purpose. And the sign of a good sitter is someone who can cope with the accidents."

Oh, boy. What a relief. I grinned. "I'll never forget the look on your face when Jackie spilled that juice."

"I'll never forget the look on your face when the jar got stuck on his hand!"

"And . . . I'll never forget the look on your face when Jackie knocked you into me." (Mary Anne turned beetroot-red.) "Oh, no. It was a *nice* look. Really nice. You know, you have a pretty smile," I said in a rush.

This turned Mary Anne speechless again, but she flashed me that gorgeous smile. And that did it. There and then I silently thanked my parents for deciding to leave Louisville, and for bringing me here to Stoneybrook to meet Mary Anne Spier, the first girl I ever fell in love with. (Okay, maybe I was just in *like* with her, since we were only in eighth grade, but that was good enough for me.)

My letter to Mary Anne ended:

AND THAT IS MY MOST VIVID
MEMORY — MOVING HERE, SHOWING
OFF MY BABYSITTING SKILLS,
AND FALLING FOR YOU.

LOVE YA FOR EVER,

LOGAN

Mallory

15th CHAPTER

Mallory
X

saturday

Dear Miss. Moody,

Hi! My name is Mallory Pike and I'm ten years old. I have seven brothers and sisters. Three of them are identical triplets. (They are boys.) Do you get a lot of letters from kids who have so many brothers and sisters, triplets included? Probably not.

Anyway, the real reason I'm writing is to tell you you're my favourite author. And I guess I am your favourite fan. I just love your books. I've been reading them for two years now. The best one (in my opinion) was <u>Nitty Gritty Meatballs</u>. That was so funny. I read part of it to my brother Nicky while he was having a snack, and he laughed so hard milk shot out of his nose . . . .

Last year, when I was ten, Amelia Moody was my favourite author. She writes really funny books— like the meatball book—and I wanted to tell her so (although the letter had not been my idea). I found this rough draft of my letter to her in a box of stuff I saved. I was looking through the box after Kristy's slumber party, trying to decide on my most vivid memory. When I saw the letter, I knew in a flash what my memory was. And it involved Amelia Moody. (By the way, when I sent her the final draft of the letter, I took out the part about Nicky's nose and the milk. I didn't want to make her feel sick.)

When I think how different my life was just over a year ago, I am amazed. The time I am talking about was actually about sixteen months ago. Sixteen months ago I was ten. The triplets were nine, Vanessa was eight, Nicky was seven, Margo was six, and Claire was four. That might not seem so different, but here's the catch: I was not a babysitter yet. I was still a babysittee. Mary Anne and Kristy and the other older members of the club were still coming over to our house and sitting *for* me. I was not sure how I felt about that. I loved seeing all those girls, and I loved that they let me help them babysit, but I was a little embarrassed to have to be sat for by them. Still, when I was not yet babysitting for real, I had lots more free time for things such as reading. And writing letters to authors, although as I

144

mentioned, that letter was not my idea. It was Mary Anne's. So I suppose I have Mary Anne to thank for my most vivid memory.

The idea for the letter came on a bright, early spring day . . .

"Mal?" Mum called up the stairs to me. "Honey?"

"I'm reading!" I called back. That was a standard reply for me.

"Mary Anne and Claudia are going to be here any minute."

"Okay!"

I knew why Mum was telling me that. It was because I idolized my babysitters. She knew I'd want to come downstairs when they arrived.

And I did. I also wanted to get to a really good stopping place in *Mandy Madango Takes the Bull By the Horns* before I ventured out of my room. *Mandy Madango* was my latest Amelia Moody book, although it was not *her* latest book, since it had been written nine years earlier. But it was the one I was currently reading, and I had been looking for it for months. It had been hard to find in the bookshop, and it was constantly on loan from both the school library and the public library. Finally I had put myself on a waiting list for it at the school library. The day before, Friday, the librarian had stopped me in the corridor of Stoneybrook Elementary and said to

145

me, "Good news, Mallory. *Mandy Madango* was just returned, and your name is next on the list. I'll hold the book for you until the end of the day."

The end of the day? I wanted the book right then. So I turned on my heel and followed Mrs Swallow to the library. She was a bit surprised when she reached her desk and found me directly behind her. But she recovered and handed over the book.

I had read *Mandy Madango* after school and after dinner that day, and after breakfast this morning. Now, only three chapters were left to go. I was tempted to finish the book before I ran downstairs to see Mary Anne and Claudia. On the other hand, I didn't want the story to end. I wanted to drag it out a while longer. So at the end of the fourth to last chapter, I closed the book, sighed, and went downstairs.

I had been so wrapped up in the book that I didn't realize Mum and Dad had already left. Now I found Mary Anne entertaining my sisters in the den, while Claud kept an eye on the boys who were playing in the garden.

"Hi, Mal," said Mary Anne. "What are you reading? Your mum said you were lost in a good book upstairs."

"Oh, I was. I am. It's *Mandy Madango Takes the Bull By the Horns*."

"By Amelia Moody?" replied Mary Anne. She

grinned. "I've read all her books. They're great. They're so *funny*."

"I know. I always get completely caught up in them. It's like nothing else is happening. The only world is the world of the book I'm in."

"Some of her books are sad, too," said Mary Anne, looking dreamy. "I remember crying all the way through *The Lost Grandmother*."

"Me too!" I exclaimed. "You know what else is *really* sad? I've read all but two of Miss Moody's books now. When I read those two, I won't have any more to read. Unless a new book comes out."

"You should write to her," said Mary Anne.

"What? Write to who?"

"To whom," Mary Anne corrected me. "To Amelia Moody. Haven't you ever written to an author, Mal?"

Well, no. I hadn't. It had not occurred to me. But it was a great idea. "How would I write to her?" I asked. "I don't know her address."

"Look in the front of *Mandy Madango* to see what company published it. The address will be there, too. Send a letter to the company and someone will send it on to Amelia Moody."

"Cool," I said. But the next words out of my mouth were, "I can't write to an author!" I must have been crazy even to have thought about it.

"Why not?" asked Mary Anne.

"Because . . . I mean, what would I say to her?"

"Just what you said to me. That you like her

books. Everyone likes to be complimented. For instance, I like to hear what a smashing sitter I am."

Claire, who was sitting on Mary Anne's lap, began to giggle.

"Well," I said, "I suppose I could tell her that. But then what would I say?"

"Mm." Mary Anne frowned. "Tell her about your family. And that you like to write, too. And tell her you aren't writing for a school assignment. Authors are always receiving letters from kids whose teachers *made* them write. They probably hate that. Dozens of letters all the same. It's like getting a pile of homework papers."

"Mary Anne?" spoke up Claire. "I don't get homework yet."

"I know you don't," said Mary Anne. "Not in nursery school."

"Will I have it next year in kindergarten?"

"Probably not," replied Mary Anne.

"I had homework in kindergarten once," said Margo. "We had to collect autumn leaves so we could press them between pieces of wax paper."

"Tough assignment," said Vanessa from the floor where she was lying on her stomach, writing poetry and drawing pictures.

"Vanessa," I said warningly.

"Sorry," she answered.

"So are you going to write to Amelia Moody?" Mary Anne asked me.

I scrunched up my face. I just was not sure. "Do you think she'll answer me?" I said finally.

It was Mary Anne's turn to scrunch up her face. "I don't know."

"Did you ever write to an author?" asked Vanessa from the floor.

Mary Anne laughed. "As a matter of fact, yes."

"Why are you laughing?" I asked.

"Because I wrote to Louisa May Alcott. You know, the author of *Little Women* and *Jo's Boys*?"

I began to laugh, too, but Vanessa said, "So?"

"So she's dead," said Mary Anne. "She's been dead for years. Decades."

Vanessa looked upset. "What happened to your letter?"

"I'm not sure. I had sent it to some publishing company. And I got a really nice letter back from a person who works there. He told me how much Louisa May Alcott would have liked my letter— and then he told me she was dead! I was so, so embarrassed."

"Mary Anne—Amelia Moody *is* alive, isn't she?"

"Oh, I think so. Read the author page in the back of the book."

I *flew* upstairs. I have never got there from the den so fast. Then I grabbed the book and flew back downstairs. I opened it to the last page. It was headed "About the Author." With a great sigh of relief I read the final sentence of the page

149

aloud. "Amelia Moody currently lives in the Adirondacks with her husband. They have two sons." But then I let out a gasp. "Wait a sec! This book is nine years old. Anything could have happened in nine years."

"Do you have a more recent book?" asked Mary Anne.

"Maybe. I'll go and see. I have some paper-backs upstairs."

I flew to my room again. This time I piled my Amelia Moody books on my bed. (I had seven.) I looked in the front of each one to find out when it had been published. Then I ran downstairs with the newest one. It had been published just the year before.

"Okay," I said to Mary Anne and my sisters. "Keep your fingers crossed." Vanessa and Margo dramatically crossed all of their fingers and their eyes. (Claire struggled, but could not cross any of her fingers.) Once again I turned to the back page of the book and read the last sentence aloud. "Amelia Moody currently lives in the Adiron-dacks with her husband. They have two sons." I let out another sigh of relief. "Oh, thank goodness."

Mary Anne grinned at me. "So are you going to write to her?"

"Well . . . yes. Yes, I am," I said. (I think I had known that all along.)

I took *Mandy Madango* and Amelia Moody's

150

other book back to my room. I did not finish
Mandy Madango that day. I was too busy
composing my letter. I bet I started it a hundred
times. Each time, in my best, most careful
handwriting, I wrote "Dear Miss Moody," and
then I would pause. I thought about the things
Mary Anne had suggested I write. I thought
about not letting my note sound like a homework
assignment.

Finally I composed the first paragraph. (It was
just like the one in the draft I had found.) Then I
composed the second paragraph. (In the final
version of it, the part about Nicky's nose was
gone, and I replaced it with two sentences about
the chapter in *Nitty Gritty Meatballs* that had
made me laugh the hardest.) Then I wrote a third
paragraph telling Miss Moody about the parts in
The Lost Grandmother that made me cry the
hardest. Finally I thanked Miss Moody for
deciding to become an author. Then I ended my
letter like this:

> Your Number One Fan
> (Honest - no one is a bigger fan
> than me, and that's a fact),
> Mallory Pike

P.S. I want to be an author myself one day.

On Monday I posted the letter. I hardly dared to hope for a reply. And when two weeks went by without one, I stopped hoping. After three weeks, I tried to forget. After four weeks, I really had forgotten. And the very next day a letter with my name on it arrived in the mail. No return address was on it. I opened it curiously.

The letter was from Amelia Moody. She thanked me for my letter. I could tell hers was just a form letter, printed out on a computer. But I did not care, because after her signature she had added a P.S. in her own handwriting. It said:

P.S. On May 2nd from 12:00–2:00 p.m. I will be signing books at Books By the Dozen in Washington Mall. I think that is near Stoneybrook. Perhaps you can attend.

Perhaps? I wouldn't miss it for the world.

16th
CHAPTER

Mallory

How I survived from the day I received Amelia Moody's letter until the day of the signing is beyond me. The first weeks dragged along like the weeks before my birthday or the weeks before the last day of school. Then when—finally—only one more week was left, I suddenly thought of a thousand things. What should I wear to a book signing? (I did not know anyone who had been to one.) What should I say to Miss Moody? Should I introduce myself? Should I say, "Remember me? I'm your number one fan, the one who wrote you the letter?" Should I bring her a present? If so, what?

On Monday night, five days before the signing, I sat on my bed in the room I share with Vanessa. I had the room to myself. This was because I had

153

kicked Vanessa out. "Please, *please* do your homework in the dining room," I had said to her. "I really need some privacy."

So Vanessa had gone. She was in a daze anyway, working on a new poem. And now I was sitting and thinking. I mulled over my three questions: What should I wear? What should I say? Should I bring a present? I decided that, by far, the clothing question was the least interesting (although I did want to look nice). I tackled it first, in order to get it out of the way.

I opened our wardrobe. I looked inside. I shoved Vanessa's clothes over to the left and spread mine out a little. I should probably wear a dress, I thought. Miss Moody had included her birthdate in her letter and I had worked out that she was sixty-four years old. In general, older people like dressed-up kids. This decision, however, presented two more problems. 1. If I dressed up, how dressy should I get? Church dressy? School dressy? School photo-day dressy? I didn't want to overdo it, but I did want to please Miss Moody. 2. What if I was the only kid at the signing who knew Miss Moody's age? Would I also be the only one there who was dressed up? I solved this dilemma by deciding I'd rather please Miss Moody. Then I opted for middle-of-the-road dressy, which meant school-picture-day dressy.

And then I had a brilliant idea. I had enclosed

my school photo in the letter I had sent Miss Moody. So I decided to wear the outfit my picture had been taken in. Maybe that would jog Miss Moody's memory when she met me. Maybe she would think, Ah, you must be Mallory Pike, the number one fan who wrote me the letter.

By the time the outfit question was settled, I was exhausted. I decided to put off the next two questions until later in the week.

I tackled question number two on Wednesday. I thought that when I first saw Miss Moody maybe I should not start off with "Remember me?" just in case she didn't. I decided, instead, to say, "Hi. My name is Mallory Pike. I wrote you a letter and you wrote back. I'm the one with seven brothers and sisters. And I said I was your number one fan." Then I realized I might be a tiny bit nervous when I actually met Miss Moody. I might not be able to remember all that. So I wrote it down and memorized it. I practised it a few times. Then I practised it in front of the mirror. Then I put on my school picture outfit and practised it again. A dress rehearsal. I even added a couple of gestures. And I reminded myself to shake Miss Moody's hand.

By Friday I was ready to think about a present for Miss Moody. My options were limited. I had only four dollars. Also, I did not want to embarrass her by giving her something too splendid. On the other hand, I wanted to impress her. And I wanted the gift to express my appreciation for the books she'd written. I decided on a bouquet of flowers. I could raid our garden before I left for the signing.

When I woke up on Saturday morning I did not feel very well. My stomach was full of butterflies. I was nervous.

I am going to meet an *author* today, I said to myself. And not just any author. I am going to meet the author of my favourite books in the world. I am going to meet *Amelia Moody*, the person who thought up *Mandy Madango* and *The Lost Grandmother* and all the other stories, and who told them in a way that made me want to keep reading on and on and on, even after the book had ended.

I shivered. Then I drew in a deep breath. I had to make those butterflies go away. I did not want to be nervous while I was talking to Miss Moody. I did not want to say something silly.

At breakfast that morning, Mum said to me, "Today's your big day, honey. Are you ready for it?"

"I hope so. What time are we leaving?" I still needed to get dressed and to pick Miss Moody's bouquet.

"About eleven-thirty," replied Mum. "And

today is going to be a mother-daughter day. Just you and me."

"We're the only ones going?" I cried. This was too good to be true. Usually my family travels in a pack, like wolves.

"Just us," said Mum.

"Cool."

When breakfast was over I dressed in my school photo outfit. In case you're wondering, this was a flowered waistcoat over a pink turtle-neck with a navy skirt, navy tights, and slip-on shoes. It was not a spring outfit. It was an autumn outfit which, of course, was when our school photos had been taken. I walked sedately down-stairs in it.

"Is that what you're wearing?" Mum asked me.

I have never liked that question. It means that the person asking it does not approve of what you're wearing.

I hesitated. "Yes?"

Mum hesitated, too. Then she said, "Okay," and smiled at me. (I think that is called humouring someone.)

At half-past eleven that morning I climbed into our estate car carrying the bouquet of flowers. I slid in next to Mum.

"This is nice," she said. "A girls' day out. After the signing, why don't we have lunch and then maybe do some shopping?"

157

"Okay," I agreed. But to tell the truth, I couldn't think about anything beyond meeting Amelia Moody.

We reached the mall at noon. We found Books By the Dozen at 12.10. And when we did, I couldn't believe my eyes. I was not Miss Moody's only fan. A line of kids waiting to meet her wound around and around the shop and then stretched partway down the mall.

"I don't believe it," Mum muttered as we joined the end of the line. She checked her watch.

"We'll never get to see her!" I wailed. "She's only going to be here until two o'clock. What if they cut off the line?"

"I hope she signs books fast," said Mum.

Unbelievably, the line did move. And it moved more quickly than I had thought it would. Forty-five minutes later we were actually in the shop (although we still had a long way to go). I had had plenty of time to look at the other kids who were waiting to meet Miss Moody. They were girls and boys (maybe a few more girls than boys), and most of them were about nine, ten, eleven or twelve years old. Some of them were medium dressy, like me. But most of them were wearing jeans. I did not feel out of place, though. Anyway, no one in the shop was paying attention to what people were wearing. We were too busy looking at a display. It was a table piled high with copies of Amelia Moody's new book, *Live From New York*, which showed a picture of a kid in a TV station.

"Mum! Amelia Moody has written another book!" I cried. "Please can I buy it? I'll pay you back as soon as I can." (If I ever earned any money.)

"Okay, honey," replied Mum. "I expect this is the book she's signing, anyway."

I looked ahead of me. Nearly every kid in the line was clutching a copy of *Live From New York*, although Miss Moody's other books were for sale, too.

I took a copy from the display, opened it, and began to read. I was in the middle of the second chapter when I glanced up and saw that only about ten people stood between me and . . . Amelia Moody herself.

"Mum, there she is!" I said with a gasp. I turned to the back of the book and examined the photo of Miss Moody. "She doesn't look a bit like her photo," I whispered to Mum.

The line crept towards Miss Moody. She was sitting behind a table. A woman was sitting next to her. She was opening the books for Miss Moody to sign. A large vase of flowers sat on the table. I glanced down at my bouquet. The flowers were wilting. They looked awfully ordinary compared to the ones on the table. I stuck the bouquet behind my back.

We inched forward. The butterflies came back. To distract myself, I rehearsed my speech. "Hi,"

I said to myself. "My name is Mallory Pike. I—I—" What? What was I supposed to say next? I had forgotten the speech.

Now just four kids were ahead of me in the line. I watched the first two hand their books to Miss Moody and tell her their names. Miss Moody smiled at them. Then she scribbled something in each book. Then the kids took the books back and walked away. That was that.

The next kid stood and talked to Miss Moody while her book was being signed. She asked a million questions. Her father snapped a picture of her talking to Miss Moody.

"Bother," said Mum. "I should have brought my camera."

Finally the kid in front of me stepped up to Miss Moody. Silently he handed her his book.

"Didn't you want to ask her something?" his mother whispered loudly.

The boy blushed. "No!"

And then it was my turn. Suddenly my legs felt like water. Mum had to push me forward. I approached the table slowly.

"Hi," said Miss Moody cheerfully.

I could not answer her. My mouth had turned to sandpaper. Instead I stuck the book out. I tried to remember my speech, but I couldn't remember even the first word.

"What's your name?" Miss Moody asked me.

At the same time, Mum whispered, "Give her the flowers."

I had decided not to give her the puny old flowers, but how would Mum know that? So I held them out. And then—before I could answer Miss Moody's question, or before she could say thank you—I burst into tears. I just could not believe that I, Mallory Pike, number one fan, was standing in front of Amelia Moody, famous author.

Mum appeared at my side. "Her name is Mallory," she said gently. "M-A-L-L-O-R-Y. And she's been looking forward to meeting you."

I was afraid Mum might add, in a whisper, something embarrassing like, "She's so over-emotional." But she didn't. She put her arm around me and I stood in front of Amelia Moody with tears running down my cheeks while Miss Moody wrote in my book.

When I opened the book later—after we had left the shop—I saw what she had written: *For Mallory, a special fan. Happy Reading! Amelia Moody.*

But I could not look at the book while we were still in the shop. In fact, I could not do much of anything. When Miss Moody had finished writing, she closed my book. Then she slid it across the table. Mum picked it up for me while I continued to stand in front of the table. Miss

161

Moody smiled at me. Finally she said, "Thank you for coming, Mallory."

I wanted to say *so* many things to her. I wanted to say, "I got your letter," and "I'm wearing the outfit I wore for my school photo," and "I want to be an author, too, someday," and "I *love* your books." But I didn't. I couldn't. I couldn't even say thank you. I just left the shop with my mum.

However, I had learned something important. I had seen what an impact an author could have on a reader—the reaction she could provoke. And that was when I thought, Someday I *will* be a writer, just like Amelia Moody.

Shannon

17th CHAPTER

Shannon

SUMMER PROJECT
CREATIVE WRITING
STONEYBROOK DAY SCHOOL

THIRTEEN
BY SHANNON KILBOURNE

I had finally turned thirteen. I thought the day would never come. I had waited and waited. I had waited since I was nine. No kidding. Ever since I was nine, all I wanted was to be thirteen. Twelve seemed to go on forever. But it had ended, I had had my birthday party, and now I was . . . thirteen. It was the best present I got.

Shannon

My friends who go to Stoneybrook Middle
School weren't the only ones with a summer
assignment. Every student at Stoneybrook Day
School—from the kindergarteners on up, had
been given some sort of summer assignment.
Mine was a creative writing assignment, and
frankly we hadn't been given much direction.
The topic was up to us.

Thank goodness for the slumber party at
Kristy's house. Jessi's question that night about
your most vivid memory had made me think. And
finally it had given me the topic for my paper.
Only I didn't title the paper "My Most Vivid
Memory." My creative writing teacher hates
things like that. He says it's gimmicky. So I called
my story "Thirteen", but it was actually about a
time in my life from which I did have awfully
vivid memories.

The time was not so long ago; less than a year
ago, in fact. As you can tell from the beginning of
the story, I had finally turned thirteen—although
not so recently. That had happened months
earlier, but I thought it was a good story starter.

Eighth grade had just begun. Something you
should know about me is that I adore school. I
have always liked it. I'm clever and I work very
hard. I hope you don't think I sound conceited. I
really am clever. At the beginning of every school
year we take these tests, and I always score

166

practically off the charts. It's been that way for as long as I can remember.

Maybe that's one reason school has been so important to me. Since I'm clever, I do well. And since I do well, my teachers notice me. They give me extra assignments and special opportunities. And I take advantage of it all. I'm in a million clubs at school, and I have a lot of interests. Also, my home life is not that great. Hardly anyone knows about it. I don't talk about it much. Anyway, to forget about things, I sometimes throw myself into school.

Don't get me wrong. I live in a nice house (okay, a nice mansion) in a nice neighbourhood. My sisters and I have never lacked for anything. But I think my parents have. I don't know exactly what's wrong with their marriage, but something's missing. And a year ago I think things were especially bad between them.

I could feel the tension in the house. Sometimes the air almost seemed to vibrate with it. I used to think you could stick a tuning fork into the dining room during meal times and it would start to hum by itself. I was especially aware of things during the summer between seventh and eighth grade, so I was looking forward to the start of school more than usual. School would be my escape, my safe haven.

Can you believe I almost gave part of that up?

Shannon

And all because of a new girl named Sally White. How could I have been so shallow? Okay, maybe I wasn't shallow. But I certainly didn't have my priorities straight.

On the first day of school, Tiffany and Maria and I dressed in our school uniform, the hot weather version. Then we hurried downstairs. That was the one day of the year we could guarantee we'd be on time. By the second day, the novelty of school would have worn off for Tiffany, who did not particularly share my feelings about school. We would have to prod her and coax her and occasionally threaten her with the idea of missing the bus and having to walk three miles to school.

But on the first day of school we bounded into the kitchen with time to spare. A good thing, too, because Mum wanted to perform her first-day-of-school ritual.

"Oh, don't you three look sweet," she said as we stood in a row before her in our matching outfits.

"Thanks," said Tiffany.

"Okay, let me get the camera."

"Can't we eat first?" whined Maria, who could be an effective whiner.

Tiffany had already taken her place at the dining room table, so Mum relented. "All right. Breakfast first, then the photo."

The photo was, as you've probably guessed, a

back-to-school photo. Mum took one of my sisters and me every year. The funny thing about the photos was that since Mum always posed us in the same spot, and we were always wearing the same outfits, the pictures looked nearly identical year after year. (I once arranged the photos in chronological order, from earliest to most recent, and zoomed through them like one of those "flip books", hoping to see us age, but it didn't really work.)

Mum hurried us through breakfast. She was just dying to get out her new camera. She posed Tiffany and Maria and me on the front steps. She snapped our picture, then two more "just in case." And then my sisters and I stood by our drive waiting for our bus. (I just know Mum was watching us from the front door.) The bus arrived, ground to a halt, and we climbed on.

"Hey, you lot!" I cried. My group of friends— Polly, Lindsey, Greer, and Meg—were in the last two seats, just where they had said they'd be sitting, and I struggled towards them as the bus lurched down the street.

Polly and Greer were sitting in one seat and had saved the seat in front of them for me. Lindsey and Meg were in the other seat, and were talking so intently to another girl that they didn't even notice me when I sat down.

I had never seen that other girl.

I leaned over my seat, tugged on Polly's sleeve,

and whispered to her, "Who's that?" I jerked my thumb towards the girl.

"Her name is Sally White. She's new. She's in our grade."

"Oh." I turned around to check on Tiffany and Maria, saw that they'd found seats with friends, then turned back to my own friends. Since Lindsey and Meg still hadn't greeted me, I said pointedly to them, "Hi, you two. Did you have a nice summer?"

Meg finally tore herself away from Sally White. "Oh. Hi, Shannon," she said.

"Hi, Shannon," Lindsey echoed. "This is Sally White. Sally, this is Shannon Kilbourne. She's in our grade, too."

Sally looked me up and down. She narrowed her eyes. Why did she seem so critical? Below my neck was nothing but yet another Stoneybrook Day School uniform. Finally Sally squeezed out a hi. Then she turned back to Lindsey and Meg.

The bus ride to school took about half an hour, what with all the stopping and starting and winding through neighbourhoods. I did not speak to Sally again. In fact, I spoke only to Polly and Greer. But I kept my eye on Sally, Lindsey, and Meg. And I noticed something interesting. By the time the bus pulled up in front of school, Lindsey was staring out of the window, and only Meg and Sally were talking. When the driver opened the doors of the bus, Sally jumped up and

170

linked her arm through Meg's, and the two of them walked away together. Lindsey scuffed along after Polly and Greer and me.

"What was all that about?" I asked Lindsey, my eyes following Sally and Meg.

Lindsey shrugged. "I'm not sure."

At lunchtime, Sally and Meg sat by themselves and whispered behind cupped hands. Lindsey and Polly and Greer and I sat nearby, watching.

"You'd think Meg had a new best friend," said Greer.

"You would, wouldn't you?" agreed Lindsey sourly.

Lindsey and Greer and Polly talked and worried about Meg all day. I was interested—but I was more interested in school things. I loved the classes I had signed up for. Apart from the usual ones, such as English and algebra, I was taking psychology and philosophy. And I was thinking about joining the astronomy club. Actually, my science teacher had invited me to join it. I would be the only eighth-grader in it. The other members were in ninth through to twelfth grade. I was flattered.

By the end of the day my friends and I were hot and sticky. Our school was air conditioned, but in the ninety-eight degree heat you almost couldn't tell. We boarded our bus, mopping at our damp faces with paper towels. Meg and Sally were already on the bus, sitting in one of the back seats. They didn't look up as Greer and Polly and Lindsey and I started down the aisle.

When we were about halfway to the back, Polly, who was leading the way, was stopped short by Greer who was right behind her. Greer was pulling on the straps of Polly's backpack. "Let's sit here," she said urgently. "Not at the back."

For as long as I could remember we had sat in the back. Those are the choice seats because they're furthest from the bus driver, and from the little kids who like to sit near her. I'm sure other kids had wanted to sit at the back, but no one ever challenged us.

Polly looked surprised. "Why not?"

Greer scowled. "Just because. You know."

Oh. Because Meg and Sally were back there. Immediately I slid into the nearest seat. I pulled Lindsey after me. Then Greer and Polly sat down across the aisle from us.

I looked back towards Sally. "What *is* it about her?" I asked. "Why is she Meg's new best friend?"

"Well, she is kind of cool," admitted Lindsey. "You should have heard the things she was telling us this morning. She's just moved here from London. She lived there for eight months. She has travelled everywhere. Her mother is some kind of film star. Sally knows all these famous people, and ... and she's gorgeous." Lindsey paused. "I kind of wish she'd chosen me."

18th CHAPTER

Shannon

Lindsey's words echoed in my head as the bus rattled through Stoneybrook. "I kind of wish she'd chosen me." *Chosen* me. Which meant, I suppose, that she had chosen Meg instead. But chosen her for what? For her best friend, since she was new in school and needed a friend? But she could have been friends with *all* of us. She could have started her year at SDS with four friends, instead of just one. And why Meg? Why *was* Meg the chosen one?

In school the next day Meg and Sally remained a group unto themselves.

My friends watched them with horror and fascination. "Sally's got them tickets to see Bruce Springsteen in concert," said Greer, in awe. "Or I suppose her mum has. They're going this weekend."

Later, Greer dropped another titbit of information. "Sally has her own horse. She and Meg are going riding this afternoon."

I, myself, was more interested in something Mr Katz had said to me. He was my science teacher. "Will you be ready to take the test a week from Monday, Shannon?" he wanted to know.

I stared at him blankly. "Test?" I repeated.

"To join the astronomy club."

"I thought you had *invited* me to join."

"Uh-oh. No. I meant I was inviting you to take the test to join. If you want, I can lend you some books so you can do a little reading beforehand."

"Well . . . okay." I wasn't afraid of tests. Plus, I did enjoy astronomy, and I wanted very much to be a member of the club.

I spent the rest of the week and a good part of the weekend poring through the books Mr Katz lent me. But I was not too caught up in them to notice something on the school bus on Monday. Sitting in the middle seats were Lindsey, Polly, and Meg. In the back seat were Sally and Greer. I slid in next to Meg, who was looking lonely.

"Hi," I said. "Um," (I glanced back at Sally) "um, did you have fun at the concert this weekend?"

Meg became tearful. But she managed to reply,

174

"Well, I thought we were having fun. I mean, *I* was having fun. I'd never been to a big concert like that before, and Sally's mum had backstage passes and everything. It was so cool. But, well, maybe I did something wrong. I mean, I'm not as sophisticated as Sally. Every time I got excited about something—like when we'd see someone famous—and I'd say, 'Oh, my gosh! Look at him!' or 'I can't believe we're backstage!' Sally would scowl. Then she told me I was a baby. By the time we got home she almost wasn't talking to me. And today," Meg turned around slowly and looked at Greer and Sally, "well . . ." Her voice trailed off.

"Greer says Sally has her own horse," I said.

Meg brightened. "Yeah, she does. He's beautiful. His name is Sure Thing, and he's a purebred, or whatever you call it."

"Thoroughbred, I think."

"Actually, she and her parents have, like, five horses. Sometimes they race them. Sally said Sure Thing's racing days are over, though. You should see Sally's house, Shannon. I've never been in anything like it. They have such interesting things. Paintings and statues—a lot of valuable art, I suppose—and some urn we weren't allowed to touch and a sword and some tribal masks and a hairless cat."

"A hairless cat? Ugh."

175

"It was sort of disgusting. I didn't want to touch it."

Tribal masks? Hairless cats? Famous people? Valuable art? Sally did seem interesting. Actually, she seemed exotic. I was beginning to understand why everyone was so fascinated by her. I decided I wanted to know more about her—especially after Meg added that Sally's parents had put a telescope in the attic of their house.

But I did not have much of a chance to get to know Sally during the next few days. She hung around exclusively with Greer.

Now Greer's the chosen one, I thought enviously.

And she was. Until Friday night.

On Saturday morning our phone rang. I was immersed in the books from Mr Katz. I had to be ready to take the test on Monday. And I was determined to pass it. So I paid no attention to the ringing phone.

"Shannon! It's for you!" Tiffany yelled a few moments later.

"Okay!" I made my way to the extension in the hall. "Hello?" I had stars and planets on the brain.

"Hello, Shannon? This is Sally. Sally White."

It *was*? "Sally? Hi." My heart began to pound.

"Hi. What are you doing?"

"Studying. What are—"

"Why are you studying on a Saturday morning?" interrupted Sally. "You don't have to study all weekend, do you? Can you come over today?"

My pounding heart thumped even harder. "Of course! Sure I can!" I said.

And that was how, two hours later, I found myself sitting on the Whites' patio eating lunch with Sally.

I was the new chosen one.

"Let's go swimming," said Sally the moment we had finished eating.

"Right now?" I replied. "We'll get cramp."

"Oh, that's an old wives' tale," said Sally. But then she went on, "Want to see the rest of our house?"

"Okay. Where's the hairless cat?"

"Tallahassee? I don't know."

"Your cat's name is Tallahassee?"

"Mum named her. She gets to name everything." Sally began leading me through room after room.

"Look at all this cool stuff," I kept saying. "Hey, where's the telescope? Meg said you have one."

"In the attic. But telescopes are boring."

"Not to me. Please can we see it?"

Sally sighed. She led me to the attic. "There it is."

"Cool." I told Sally about being asked to join

the astronomy club. "The test is on Monday," I added. "In fact, I'm going to have to leave soon. I have to keep studying."

"No! You can't. We haven't gone swimming yet."

"But I didn't even bring my swimming costume."

"You can borrow one of mine."

And that was the beginning. That was the beginning of how I almost blew the astronomy club. I stayed at Sally's all afternoon. I did manage to study that night. But early on Sunday, Sally called me again. "Want to come over, Shannon? You can ride Sure Thing."

"Sally, I told you, the astronomy test is tomorrow. Today is my last chance to study for it. Can't I come over sometime next week? After the test? The club is really important to me."

"How important?"

"I—I don't know. Just . . . really important."

"So important that you're going to study all day?"

"I—"

"Think it over and call me back."

Do you know what? I really did think it over. For far too long. I wasted more than an hour in my room.

This was the thing about Sally. None of us knew her very well, but she was so glamorous that we wanted to be chosen by her. Being chosen by her mattered.

But getting into the astronomy club mattered more to me. I called Sally back. "I have to study," I told her. "See you tomorrow. 'Bye."

Sally just hung up.

I went on ploughing through those books. I was just barely going to finish studying and have time for my weekend homework. As it was, I was not sure I would pass the test.

When the bus reached our house the next morning, I climbed aboard hesitantly. I wondered what the seating arrangement would be. This was it: hovering somewhere in the middle of the bus were Greer, Meg, and Lindsey. In the back seat were Polly and Sally.

I was out, Greer was out, Meg was out. Polly was the new chosen one.

I could not think about Sally any more. Or about the confused, disturbed faces of the girls who were not chosen. I opened one of the books from Mr Katz and concentrated.

That afternoon I passed the test. Actually, I aced it. Mr Katz's words later were that I would be "an asset to the astronomy club."

By Thursday, Polly was no longer the chosen one. The new chosen one was a sixth-grader named Frannie.

"What about me?" wailed Lindsey. "She never chose me. She chose everyone else in our group, but not me. And now she's chosen a *sixth*-grader. What's wrong with me?"

Shannon

You're probably lucky, I thought.

I tried not to feel bitter. I tried to feel glad about the astronomy club. But every time I stepped on to the school bus and saw Sally with some other chosen girl, angry feelings washed over me. Soon those feelings washed over me at home, at school . . . I felt angry all the time. And when I noticed Kristy Thomas, who was the new girl in our neighbourhood then, I was not nice to her. I was not inclined to be nice to *any* new girl, not after the way Sally had treated my friends and me. It took a long time for my anger to drain away. When it finally did, I realized how foolish *I* had been. I vowed never to let myself be drawn to someone like Sally White again, someone who would take me away from myself. *I* would choose my friends, then let them decide if they wanted to be *my* friends. A two-way street. And for my next new friend, I chose Kristy.

Dawn

19th CHAPTER

Dawn

Tuesday

Dear Mary Anne, Kristy,
   Stacey, Jessi, Shannon,
   Logan, Claud, and Mal,

   Hello from California! I'm
sending this letter to Claud's
house, hoping you will read
it together at a club meeting.
Mary Anne wrote to me
about your slumber party,
which I'm really sorry I
missed, and about the game
you played. I know you've
been trying to come up with
your most vivid memories,
so I decided to think of mine.

183

Dawn

I don't know how long it took you guys to settle on one, but it took me all of about a second. Absolutely nothing is as vivid for me as when my parents were about to get divorced. Of course, I wouldn't forget that time anyway, but I really feel as if, right now, I could transport myself back then and remember every single second of those months. That's how vivid the divorce is ....

When I was twelve I must have been pretty naive. I thought my life would never change. I don't mean I thought I'd be twelve for ever, or that I wouldn't go on to high school and grow up and maybe have a family of my own. I just mean I thought my life would be Mum and Dad and Jeff and me living in our house in California for a long, long time.

Seventh grade had recently started and seemed

to be going fine. Jeff was nine and in fourth grade and seemed to like it. This was a relief, since he had had a bit of trouble in third grade. Nothing major. He just kept complaining of stomach aches in the morning and not wanting to leave the house. But in fourth grade, so far so good.

I was starting to babysit a lot more. My best friend Sunny liked to sit, too, and since we had turned twelve we were being offered more jobs. In school, my teachers said I would be on the honours roll by the end of the year if I kept my grades up.

My life was not perfect, though, and the flaw was my parents. Not that they were bad parents. In fact, compared to my friends' parents, I thought they were pretty cool. Even Mum, who was a total scatterbrain. The flaw was that my parents seemed to be arguing a lot. I kept trying to think back to a year earlier or even just six months earlier. Had they argued so much then? The answer was no. They were arguing more and more. Mostly they argued over little things.

For instance, one morning that autumn, Dad entered the kitchen and peered at the frying pan Mum was standing over.

"Morning," said Mum.

"Morning," replied Dad.

(I thought, Didn't they used to call each other dear or darling or something?)

Then Dad, still looking in the pan, said, "What's that?"

"Scrambled eggs."

"But I don't like scrambled eggs."

"You used to."

"Well, I don't any more. Can't you poach me an egg?"

"Poach it yourself," said Mum. She threw an oven glove on to the counter and marched out of the kitchen.

Jeff and I looked at each other. We shrugged.

Then one Saturday they had an argument during dinner. (Why did they choose mealtimes for their fights?) It started with something simple. Mum said to Dad, "Let's go to the cinema tonight."

(Goody, I thought. That meant a job for me. I could sit for Jeff.)

But Dad replied, "Oh, Sharon, not tonight."

"Why not? What do you want to do?"

"I don't know."

"You want to go out with your friends again, don't you?"

"Well—"

"Fine. Go ahead. Have fun."

As you can probably imagine, things were pretty frosty after that. Mum and Dad didn't talk during the rest of the meal. Then, the moment everyone seemed to have stopped eating, Dad jumped up from the table and headed for the door.

"Are you leaving *now*?" asked Mum, breaking the silence.

"Yup."

"You couldn't stay another moment or two and help clear up, could you?"

Dad opened his mouth to say something. He looked very put-upon.

"No, of course not. I can see that would be far too much trouble for you," Mum said. "Go ahead. Go on out and have fun."

These were the kinds of arguments they were having. They were the kinds of little arguments people have all the time, and never think twice about. Except that that autumn they had so *many* of them. After a while, a theme developed. Actually, it was more like a chain of events. Mum and Dad would argue and Mum would accuse Dad of staying out all the time. She said he was never at home. He was either working or off with his friends. Then they would argue about it, and Dad would say, well, if they were just going to argue, what was the point of his being at home? And he would go out, and then Mum would have more ammunition.

That was how it was at first.

In November, things took a different direction.

I remember the day when our lives seemed to

187

veer completely off course. I didn't see it that way then, but looking back now I do.

It started on a normal weekday. A Wednesday. My family woke up as usual and ate breakfast in the kitchen. Mum and Dad had a tiff over something. Jeff and I barely noticed. I was studying for a test and Jeff was digging around in a cereal box trying to find some free gift and anyway Mum and Dad always had tiffs.

This one ended with Dad storming out of the kitchen and Mum saying, "How late are you going to be *tonight . . . dear?*" As if he were late every single night of his life, and as if dear were the worst thing she could call him.

Dad replied, "Late enough," then left.

Jeff and I finally looked at each other. We shrugged. We didn't know what he meant, but we'd barely been paying attention, so maybe we'd missed something.

My brother and I went off to school and put in our days there. (I got an A– in the test.) After school, Jeff played at a friend's house, and I babysat for Clover and Daffodil Austin. I decided to walk them to the school playground, and Sunny came along.

By the time my job was over and I returned home, it was half-past five. Jeff was home, too, and so was Mum. Dad wasn't, but he usually didn't show up until six, especially if the traffic was bad. At half-past six he wasn't home either, but we'd heard about an incredible traffic jam and thought Dad might be caught in it. By seven, when he still wasn't home (and the traffic jam reportedly had cleared up), Mum began getting worried about dinner. She fidgeted around the kitchen, put an ice-cube tray in the oven, got out a knife when she was looking for the greaseproof paper, and poured Jeff a glass of tonic water when he asked for milk. Now, as I've said, Mum is completely scatterbrained, so this behaviour wasn't too unusual. But she seemed nervous on top of her scatterbraininess.

"Mum? What's the matter?" I asked.

Her reply was a string of muttered phrases about people who didn't have the decency to call, and about ruining perfectly good meals.

"I'm hungry," Jeff said.

"Then we are going to eat," Mum replied decisively.

And we did.

By the time Jeff and I went to bed that night, Dad still had not come home. I was worried. "What if he's been in a car accident?" I asked.

"The police would have called us," Mum replied. "He'll be home soon."

Guess what. I don't think my father came home at all that night. He was not at breakfast the next morning. When I asked where he was, Mum just said, "Out." So I didn't ask any more questions.

I wondered about him off and on during school that day. Then at six o'clock in the evening he strode through our door, so I stopped worrying. But then another weird thing happened. That night I didn't feel well. I woke up with an upset stomach. I wasn't terribly sick, but I wanted to drink something to settle my stomach. Maybe some herb tea. So I tiptoed downstairs, trying not to turn on lights or do anything else that would wake my family.

Creep, creep, tiptoe, tiptoe, CRASH!

"Ow!" I cried.

"Dawn?" said my mother's voice with a gasp.

I switched on a light. My mother was sleeping on the sofa bed in the living room, and I'd tripped over it.

"What are you doing here?" I said. I grabbed my throbbing foot.

"I—I—I wasn't, um, feeling well, and I didn't want to bother your father, so I thought I'd sleep out here."

"Oh," I replied. "I don't feel well, either. We must have a bug or something."

Maybe Mum did have a bug, but I don't think so. She slept on the couch for the next two nights, and she seemed perfectly fine in between. I wasn't supposed to know she was sleeping on the couch. She would get up early to make the sofa bed into a sofa again, but once I saw her pillow tossed in a corner of the living room, and the next

190

morning I saw a corner of the sheet sticking out of the couch.

I began to feel extremely uneasy. Why were Mum and Dad sleeping in separate rooms? I knew that was not right.

Then, early in December, something much worse happened. It was very late one night, and I was in a deep sleep. But I was woken by shouting. From my parents' bedroom I heard Mum yell, "You are a *liar*! Don't you understand? I *know* when you're lying. I catch you in your lies. And I will not have that in my house. I do not tolerate lying."

"Fine. I'll leave!" was Dad's reply. He yelled it so loudly I swear the walls vibrated. Then I heard thumps, and drawers opening and closing, and finally a door slam that was so loud I thought it would knock the house down.

Dad had left. He did not return for three days. (During that time, Jeff's stomach aches returned, and he missed school.) When Dad finally did show up, he talked to Mum for a long time in their bedroom. The next day, my parents found Jeff and me and sat us down in the living room.

"We have to talk to you," Dad said.

20th CHAPTER

Dawn

Well, maybe *you* know what my parents were going to say to Jeff and me, but I sure didn't. I did not have a clue. I would not have been any more surprised if Dad had said, "Dawn, Jeff, I have to tell you something. I've been going to clown school and I've decided to join the circus."

What he actually said was, "Dawn, Jeff, your mother and I have been talking—"

"Arguing," Jeff interrupted.

"Please let me finish," said Dad.

"I don't think I want you to," I said in a small voice. But of course he continued anyway. He had to.

"Your mother and I have been talking," Dad said, "and arguing," he added, glancing at Jeff, "and we have decided something."

192

I think Jeff knew what was coming before I did, because he clapped his hands over his ears then. Dad prised them off.

"We have decided to separate and get divorced."

I jumped to my feet. "Nooo!" I howled.

"I'm sorry, honey," said Dad.

I glared at Mum. "This is all *your* fault," I shouted at her.

"What—" she started to reply.

"It *is*. You yell at Dad, you accuse him of things, and then you tell him to leave. I heard you! I wouldn't want to be married to you either!"

"Dawn!" said my mother with a gasp.

At the same time, Dad grabbed me by the wrist and jerked me down so that I had to sit on the couch again. "Now just a minute," he said. "This is *not* your mother's fault. It is a decision we reached together. Our feelings are mutual. Maybe I *don't* want to be married to her any more, but she doesn't want to be married to me, either."

I was too angry to pay a lot of attention to what Dad was saying. I focused on one thing—"It is a decision we reached together—" and pounced on it. "Why can't you try to work things out? That's what you always tell Jeff and me to do. Work things out."

"Honey, we've tried," said Mum.

"And anyway, what can't you work out?"

Mum and Dad sighed.

"You name it," said Dad.

"We don't agree on anything," added Mum. "Money, our lifestyle, raising you kids, even where to go on holiday."

"I don't *care* where we go on holiday," wailed Jeff. "And my stomach hurts." He looked as if he were going to be sick.

Mum pulled him on to her lap and rubbed his stomach.

"And that's only half the list," said Dad.

"No, it's just about complete," said Mum.

"It's complete if you don't mind leaving out the most important—"

"Thank you so much for correcting me in front of the children," said Mum.

"So now that's a problem, too? I correct you in front of the children?"

"I'm *not* a *child*!" cried Jeff.

"Enough!" My father held up his hands. "Everyone be quiet. Dawn, do you see what your mother and I mean? We do argue about everything."

"Well, Jeff and I argue pretty often, but we still love each other. . . . Well, we *do*," I said when I saw the disgusted look on my brother's face. "Because we're brother and sister."

194

"It's a little bit different with husbands and wives," said Mum gently.

"Our lawyers will cite irreconcilable differences in the divorce proceedings," added Dad. "Despite them, we are going to try to make the divorce as amicable as possible. For your sake and Jeff's."

"Thanks a lot," I muttered.

"What's going to happen to us?" asked Jeff. "I mean, who will we live with?"

"I'm going to have primary custody of you and Dawn," replied Mum.

"And I'm going to move out for a while," said Dad. "I'll stay at a hotel. I'll be very near by."

"Why do you have to stay at a hotel?" asked Jeff. "Can't you stay here?"

Jeff did not understand a thing. "They're *get*ting a di*vorce*," I said crossly. "The whole point is that they can't get along and they don't want to be together. One of them has to move out."

"But to a hotel?" said Jeff. "You can't stay in a hotel for ever. After the hotel what are you going to do?"

Dad rubbed his eyes. "I don't know. Let's just get through the next few days. Right now I need to pack."

"Can I come with you to the hotel?"

"Jeff, no," said Dad, sounding irritated.

Jeff got off Mum's lap. He stormed off to his room.

Dawn

I glared at my parents. Then I went to my room, too.

Three days later, Mum and Jeff and I were eating lunch. We were eating on our laps in the living room. The house was a royal mess. I don't think anything, including food, had been put away for the past three days. And none of us cared. We didn't care much about eating, either. But we felt we ought to try.

Halfway through this silent meal, Mum said, "Kids, I have something else to tell you." Her voice shook slightly.

"Oh, lord. What now?" I replied.

"Dawn, don't make this any more difficult than it already is."

"Sorry."

"I have decided," said Mum very slowly, "after much thought, to move back to Stoney-brook, Connecticut, where Granny and Pop-Pop are."

"You're moving to Connecticut?" I cried. I dropped my fork, and it clattered on to my plate, then on to the floor.

"Yes," replied Mum. "We all are. I mean, you and Jeff and I are, since I have custody of you. I've talked to Dad about this. He's not thrilled, but he understands. We'll be leaving in a few weeks. Then Dad will move back here. He'll stay

196

in the house." Mum was having trouble looking at Jeff and me.

Jeff, who had not said much since Mum and Dad had told us about the divorce, now jumped to his feet. I suppose he forgot about the plate of food on his lap, because it fell to the floor, scattering cherries and the crusts of his sandwich. The plate cracked in half. "I am not moving!" he shouted. "I am staying right here. You can't make me move!"

"Honey, I don't want to have to put things this way," said Mum, "but as a matter of fact, yes I can make you move."

Jeff was in a rage. I was more practical. "Where are we going to live?" I asked. "With Granny and Pop-Pop?"

"Maybe for just a little while at first. But we're going to have our own house there. Granny and Pop-Pop are helping me find a nice house, one that will be perfect for us."

"*This* house is perfect for us," said Jeff.

I think the worst few days of my life followed that conversation. I had been too embarrassed to tell Sunny my parents were getting divorced. (I don't know why I was embarrassed. I just was.) Now I had to tell her about it, and tell her I was moving three thousand miles away, too. We wouldn't be able to babysit together any more, we wouldn't be able to walk to school together any more, and we wouldn't be able to do all of the other things we'd been doing together since second grade. How was I going to tell her that?

I had no idea. But I was going to have to tell her. And soon.

I gave myself a day to calm down. Then on Sunday afternoon I rang the Winslows' bell. Mrs Winslow answered it, and said I could go to Sunny's room. I found Sunny at her desk, studying for a test.

"I suppose I should have called before I came over," I said.

"Why?" replied Sunny. "We never call first. I can finish studying tonight."

I sat on the edge of Sunny's bed. All morning I had been planning how I would break the news to Sunny. But the moment I sat down, I burst into tears, which was not part of the plan.

"Dawn? What's wrong?" asked Sunny. She left her desk and sat beside me.

"Something awful is going on at my house," I managed to say.

Sunny looked shocked. "What?"

"Mum and Dad are getting a divorce."

"Oh, no." Sunny put her arms around me.

"But that's not the worst part. Or maybe it is," I wailed against her shoulder. "Anyway, there's more. Mum is moving back to Connecticut and she's taking Jeff and me with her."

198

"What?" Sunny pulled away from me. "You're leaving?"

I nodded. "In a few weeks."

Sunny and I spent most of the afternoon crying. We were sad, but we were angry, too. In fact, we were furious with my parents. Especially my mum.

In January, Mum began packing for our move. Let me tell you, dividing up a house is not easy. Every time Dad came over to help, he and Mum argued over who should get what and why. I escaped to Sunny's a lot. During one of my visits she announced, "I've decided to give you a going-away party."

"Really?" I was momentarily distracted from thoughts of my parents arguing.

"Yeah. We'll have it here right before you leave. We'll invite anyone you want. And we'll have whatever food you want."

You would think that would be the beginning of a great party. And it might have been. Except for one thing. I had only invited my closest friends, and as soon as we were together, we started to cry. All eight of us. We couldn't stop. Everything just made us cry harder. Mrs Winslow brought us the veggie pizza we'd ordered, and we sobbed. My friends gave me the goodbye card they'd made, and we sobbed harder. We tried to watch a video together, and we sobbed even harder.

199

Finally Sunny said, "I suppose we'd better say goodbye to Dawn." And we left Sunny's house, melting in tears.

That night I slept in my room one last time. Even though Dad had been clear that it would *always* be my room, and it would be there for me whenever I visited, I knew it wouldn't feel the same again. That night ended a chapter in my life. When I awoke the next morning, a new one began.

I was on my way to Stoneybrook, Connecticut.

21st
CHAPTER

Dawn

The removal van had left with our half of the furniture several days earlier. Thursday was the day Mum and Jeff and I were leaving California. Friday was the day the van was supposed to turn up in Stoneybrook. Which is why we were going to spend our first night in Connecticut at Granny and Pop-Pop's house.

Jeff and I were not in good moods. We had been in bad moods from the moment we woke up that morning.

"Why don't you try to make your last few hours here a little pleasanter?" Mum asked us at breakfast.

Dad had come over early that morning so the four of us could eat together before we left for the airport. We were sitting around, picking at our food. Jeff and I were sniping at each other.

Later, when Mrs Winslow pulled up in her car (she and Sunny were going to drive us to the airport), Jeff and I were so angry we could barely say goodbye to Dad. Finally Mum just said to him, "The kids will call when we get to my parents' house," and Dad nodded.

I did manage to say goodbye to Sunny, though. In the airport, we clung to each other and cried. Jeff watched us, horrified. A few minutes later we boarded the plane. I barely remember the flight. It's the only part of my vivid memories that isn't vivid at all. I suppose because it was the actual transition between my old life, which I did not want to leave behind, and my new life, which I did not want to face. Why couldn't I have just found some giant magical clock, turned time back about a year, and stayed in California? That was all I wanted.

When Mum and Jeff and I stepped off the plane, Granny and Pop-Pop were waiting for us. Usually when we see each other after a long separation, my grandparents start exclaiming things like, "Look at you! I'm so glad to see you! Oh, you've got so *big*! Dawn, you're so grown-up!"

This time they just held out their arms and hugged us wordlessly. Then we walked outside to their car. Granny began talking on the drive to Stoneybrook, though. "Wait till you see the

202

house we've found for you," she said to Jeff and me. "You're going to love it."

"Mum showed us pictures," replied Jeff.

"Oh, pictures don't do it justice. You need to see it for yourself. It's old—"

"Probably falling apart," said Jeff under his breath.

"—with a lot of history. I believe it used to be part of the Underground Railroad." (Jeff didn't know what that meant, and he didn't bother to ask.) "It was built in seventeen ninety-five," Granny added.

"Maybe we'll drive past it this afternoon so you can take a look at it," said Pop-Pop.

We did do that. To my surprise, I liked the house. It was very different from our house in California, but that was okay. I thought it had charm. And I liked the fact that it had history. If it was as old as Granny had said, maybe it even had a ghost.

That night, the time change set in. Jeff and I did not feel tired. Our biological clocks were telling us it was three hours earlier. We were practically bouncing around our grandparents' house. And all I wanted to do was phone Sunny and talk to her for about five hours.

"*Please* can I phone Sunny?" I begged Mum. "Please?"

"Honey, no. Not from here. I don't want

Granny and Pop-Pop to have to pay for a long-distance call."

"Then let's reverse the charges."

"No! I don't want the Winslows to have to pay either."

"Aren't Sunny and I ever going to be allowed to talk?" I whined. (I knew I was being a pest.) "You've already taken my father away from me. Are you going to take Sunny away, too?"

I honestly thought my mother was going to slap me then. She certainly looked as if she wanted to. And I was certainly being rude enough. Instead, she spun around and left the room. She didn't talk to me until the next day, and I can't say I blame her.

I was left in the living room with Granny. (Pop-Pop and Jeff were watching TV in another room.) I could feel her looking at me. I thought, actually, that she might be glaring at me, but when I finally dared to glance at her, I saw that her eyes had filled with tears.

She held out her arms to me. "Come here, sweetheart," she said.

I crawled on to Granny's lap as if I were a little girl again. I started to sob. I think that's why I had wanted to call Sunny. I needed to cry with someone. Granny held me tight. She did not mention what I had said to Mum. But later, I heard her knock on Mum's door, and then they had a long talk, and Mum cried, too.

By the next day, we all felt a little better. We drove to the new house just before lunchtime. The removal van had arrived.

"Boy," I said to Jeff. "Half a houseful of furniture sure looks like a lot of stuff."

"Yeah," said Jeff. He kicked at a rock. Then he added, "Jeez, it's cold."

"Don't say jeez," said Granny.

I expected Jeff to mutter, "*You* just said it." But he didn't. He jammed his hands in his pockets.

"It is cold, though," I said.

"We'll have to get some winter clothes," replied Mum.

"Well, come on. Let's give the removal men a hand." Pop-Pop was ready to spring into action.

We spent the next few hours hauling boxes around the house. We could have been organized about that. Granny and Pop-Pop are relatively organized people. And heaven knows I am. I have to be organized, what with living with Mum. (If one of us wasn't organized who knew what would happen. We might have boarded a plane to Australia instead of Connecticut.) But we felt that Mum should be in charge that afternoon, and so . . . we weren't organized.

At about six o'clock, Mum said to her parents, "Why don't you two go on home now? You've done more than enough."

Granny agreed to this very quickly, so I knew she was tired.

Mum and Jeff and I were alone in our new house in our new town in our new state in our new lives.

"What are we going to eat for dinner?" asked Jeff. (He knew the refrigerator was empty.)

"Hmm. Good question," replied Mum.

Nobody wanted to go outside in that freezing cold air again, but when Mum realized we didn't even have milk or cereal for breakfast the next morning, she decided we'd better go to the grocery shop.

So we did. And while we were out, we picked up a pizza. We ate in front of the TV set. Nobody said much. Not until bedtime. At ten o'clock, Mum went into her room, Jeff went into his room, and I went into my room. By 10.05 we were all in Mum's room.

"I heard something outside my window," said Jeff.

"There *must* be ghosts in a two hundred-year-old house," I said. "*Some*one must have died in here. Or—"

Mum put her finger on my lips. "Enough, Dawn. You're scaring Jeff."

"He's already scared."

"Well, anyway, just this once you two can sleep in here with me. But tomorrow night, back to your own beds."

We spent most of Saturday and Sunday trying to organize the house. At three on Sunday afternoon, though, Mum suddenly realized that Jeff and I might freeze the next day when we started school, so she found a clothes shop that was open, rushed us in there, and bought us parkas and gloves and hats in record time.

"Are you nervous about school tomorrow?" Jeff asked me on the way home. He was looking uncomfortable in his brand-new clothes.

"Who, me? No way."

I was scared senseless.

If I had known what was going to happen during my first week at Stoneybrook Middle School, I wouldn't have been scared at all. By the end of the second day I had made a friend. The first day, truthfully, wasn't so great, though. I was every bit as friendless as you might expect a kid who transfers to a new school in the middle of the year to be. But that changed at lunchtime on Tuesday.

I was walking through the cafeteria carrying my tray and the hot lunch. The hot lunch, by the way, looked absolutely revolting. Why, you might ask, had I not brought a lunch from home? The answer was simple. Our house was such a mess I couldn't find any of the things I'd need in order to pack a lunch. The kitchen things weren't even in the kitchen. They weren't anywhere logical. So I was forced to buy lunch.

Anyway, I was walking around with my tray looking for a place to sit down when I spotted a girl sitting at a table all by herself.

Ah-ha! What luck. I'd found another new kid. We could band together and become best friends.

Well, we did band together and become best friends, but she wasn't a new kid. She was Mary Anne. And she was sitting by herself because she'd had a huge argument with her friends—Kristy, Claudia, and Stacey. They were all cross with each other, and all sitting separately, although Mary Anne was the only one sitting alone. Mary Anne was really nice to me. She told me about SMS and the kids there. Then we realized we lived near each other. By the time lunch was over, I'd invited Mary Anne to my house the next afternoon.

Not too long after that Mary Anne and I realized that her dad and my mum had dated in high school. Not too long after *that* Mary Anne and her friends made friends again, and I was a member of the Babysitters Club. And not too long after *that* Mary Anne and I became stepsisters.

When my parents were going through the divorce, I had thought it was the worst time in my life. But look what it led to. And now—funny—here I am back in California with my dad and Jeff. And Sunny. And missing Mary Anne and Mum and Richard and Granny and Pop-Pop. But all things change. I know that now. I'll be back in Stoneybrook soon.

Mary Anne

22nd CHAPTER

Mary Anne

Saturday Night

Dear Dawn,

We have all been talking about our most vivid memories, but I've been having trouble deciding on mine. Maybe this is because a person's most vivid memory isn't necessarily her most important memory. Who knows what makes a memory vivid? Anyway, after we read your letter I decided that, once and

213

Mary Anne

*for all, I was going to
choose a memory. And
I finally did. And
since I can't sleep, I
thought I'd write and
tell you about it . . . .*

I bet I have had more babysitters and house-keepers and mother's helps (in my case, I should say father's helps) than any kid in Stoneybrook. This is because of growing up without a mum, of course. Why my dad couldn't find one person and stick with her, I'll never know, but he couldn't. (At any rate, he didn't.)

My vivid memory, which involves a vividly memorable babysitter, is from when I was eight years old. My dad and I were living in the house on Bradford Court then, the one next door to Kristy and opposite Claudia. I was in third grade, and as shy as ever.

This is how I could sum up my life: Dad, Kristy, school, and babysitters. Endless babysitters. There were babysitters for after school, and babysitters for the evening if Dad went out or had to work late, and babysitters for nights or weekends if Dad went away on business, which he did sometimes. I got used to not knowing who to expect when I walked through our door. And some of the sitters were WEIRD. One of them ate nothing but lettuce and pecans. Another was so concerned about keeping the house neat that she lost track of me. Another taught me to play bridge and took me to bridge games with her friends. (Actually, that was fun. But it wasn't what Dad was looking for in a babysitter, so he fired her.)

Anyway, with all the strange babysitters in my house, I spent more and more time over at Kristy's. I liked going to Kristy's. I thought of the Thomases as a real family. Now, at thirteen, I know that Dad and I made a perfectly nice family by ourselves. But when I was eight, the Thomases looked good to me. Kristy had brothers. She had a dog. And she had a mother. How I wished for a mother of my very own. Mimi was sweet to me. Mrs Kishi was nice to me. And Mrs Thomas was wonderful to me. She wasn't like having a mother of my very own, but she was the next best thing. She took me shopping with Kristy. She invited me over for meals (especially when my babysitters got weird). Sometimes she even mended my clothes. I asked her things I couldn't ask my dad.

And Kristy. She was my lifesaver. I was so glad she was my best friend. Sometimes when I thought about it, I couldn't believe *I* was *her* best

215

friend. If I were Kristy I wouldn't want a crybaby for a best friend. I'd want someone more like Claudia, maybe. But Kristy and I had been best friends for as long as I could remember, and somehow I knew we would always be best friends.

I was glad Kristy and I were best friends for a lot of reasons, but the two most important ones were 1. whenever I wanted to feel a part of a bigger family I could run next door, and 2. Kristy did things I would never have done myself. Sometimes she made me do them with her. The only times I ever got in trouble, Kristy was involved. She would say, "Oh, come on. It's all right to paint your room. Your father will love it." Or, "Really, it's okay to experiment with the washing machine. I've done it before." So I'd go along with her, and the next thing I'd know, we would be in major trouble. I never would have thought of doing those things on my own, but when Kristy suggested them—well, she could be pretty persuasive. She also made them sound like an awful lot of fun. I felt I just *had* to try them.

Anyway, my vivid memory is of a weekend during third grade. My father was going to be away. He had to go to Chicago on business. He did not like to go away very often, but sometimes he couldn't help it.

"Who's going to stay with me this time?" I asked, when Dad first broke the news. "It won't be Mrs Mills, will it?"

Mrs Mills smelled only of Ivory soap. She ate pickles all day long.

"No, not Mrs Mills," said my father.

"Who then?"

We were sitting on the back porch on Saturday afternoon. It was the week before Dad's business trip. I was drinking milk and Dad was drinking coffee. We were trying to eat these ginger snaps Kristy and I had made, but they tasted like soap, possibly because Mrs Mills had helped us make them.

"I'm not sure yet," replied Dad. "I'm talking to the agency." He bit into a cookie, then took the bite *out* of his mouth, and set it and the rest of the cookie discreetly on a napkin.

"The *agency*? Oh, Dad, please. Not the agency."

"Mary Anne—"

"No, really. They only send over old ladies like Mrs Mills. The ones that smell awful and eat weird things. And they're *old*. And their lips are all dried up and their mouths look like apricots—"

"Mary *Anne*," said my father again, only this time he was losing patience. "That's quite enough. Besides, I *have* to call the agency. Where else am I going to find a sitter who can spend the weekend—an entire weekend—with you?"

"Can't I stay at Kristy's this time? Or at Claudia's?"

217

"Sweetie, I don't want to impose on their families."

"Please? Please impose just this once?"

Dad was going to answer me (and he did not look pleased), but the phone rang then. He stood up and walked into the kitchen.

While he was gone, I sampled another cookie. I spat it out. It really did taste like Ivory soap.

When Dad returned, he sat down and said, "Well, that was the agency. They think they've found someone. I'll interview her on Monday."

"Dad, I just had a thought. Marjorie is going to be my sitter after school this week. I like Marjorie." (I only liked her sort of. Marjorie was younger than most of my sitters and she had a five-month-old baby she'd bring along with her. I was not thrilled with the baby, who dribbled a lot, but at least Marjorie didn't smell funny or have an apricot mouth.) "Couldn't Marjorie stay with me this weekend? Please, Dad?"

"No, honey. Marjorie has a family. She won't want to leave them for two days. I can't ask her to do that."

"She doesn't have to say yes," I muttered. I almost added, "Besides, she could bring her family here. Or I could go to her house." But I knew I was treading close to the line.

"Mary Anne, I am going to meet a woman named Mrs Tate on Monday. I'm sure she'll be very nice. And she comes highly recommended.

218

Mary Anne

The agency only provides the best sitters. Now I don't want to hear another word about this. By the way, who made these cookies?"

"Mrs Mills," I replied smugly.

On Monday, Dad met Mrs Tate before he came home from work.

"What do her lips look like?" I asked my father. "And how does she smell?"

"Her mouth looks fine, and she smells fine, Mary Anne. She'll be here when you return from school on Friday." I must have looked pathetic, because Dad added, "It'll be *fine*, just fine. And it'll only be for two days. You can manage that, honey."

"Two days and two nights," I said.

Dad sighed. "What would make this weekend easier for you?"

Now that was a good question. I thought about it seriously. I knew better than to say, "If you weren't going away." Or, "If Mrs Tate didn't have to stay here." Finally I said, "My friends."

"Your friends?"

"Dad, could I have a slumber party on Friday night? Not a big one. Could Kristy and Claudia spend the night here? That would be really fun, and then I wouldn't mind the weekend so much."

Dad wrinkled his brow. "All right," he replied. "On Friday, Kristy and Claudia can stay over, *if* their parents give them permission. They can stay for supper, too."

219

"Oh, thank you, Dad!" I cried. I gave him a quick hug. Then I phoned my friends to tell them the news.

On Friday morning, I said goodbye to my father. I was resigned about Mrs Tate, but excited about the slumber party.

"Have a good weekend," Dad called to me as I walked across the front garden with Kristy. "And behave for Mrs Tate."

"I will. See you on Sunday. 'Bye, Dad!"

When I returned to my house that afternoon a strange car was parked in our driveway. It must have belonged to Mrs Tate.

"*What is that?*" said Kristy as we gaped at it.

It was rusty and brown, with enormous head-lights. One of the windows was missing and had been replaced with plastic sheeting which was taped to the frame. The exhaust pipe looked loose and the bumper was covered with dirty stickers.

"Oh, no," I said. "Well . . . I'd better go inside." What I really wanted to do was cry, but I was afraid if I looked like a baby Mrs Tate would say I couldn't have the slumber party.

I headed inside. "Come over at six," I called to Kristy. I opened our front door. "Hello?" I said. I had a really bad feeling about Mrs Tate. I suppose because of the car.

"Is that you, Mary Anne? I'm in the kitchen."

Mrs Tate looked exactly like all the other

220

agency ladies, right down to the apricot mouth. I couldn't work out what she smelled like, though. Some combination of things. One of them might have been vinegar.

I stood in the kitchen doorway. "Hi," I said tentatively.

"Hello, there. How was school? What grade are you in?"

"Um, third," I replied.

"Good teacher?"

"I suppose."

"Cat got your tongue?"

I never know how to answer that one. I decided to change the subject. I was hungry, I wanted a snack, and Marjorie and I had made brownies the day before. "Could I have a brownie?" I asked. I opened the tin Marjorie had put them in.

"That all depends. What are you and your friends going to eat tonight?"

"Pizza?" I hadn't given it much thought.

"Then no brownie. Tsk. Pizza and a brownie all in the same day. Far too unhealthy. You may have an apple."

I opened my mouth to protest. I closed it. I opened it again. "Pl—"

"Not another word," said Mrs Tate.

"May I go to my friend's house, please?" I asked. "She lives right next door."

"Don't you want your apple?"

"No."

221

Mary Anne

"Okay. But no snacking at your friend's house."

I stormed over to Kristy's. "She's horrible!" I cried. (My lip was trembling.) "She wouldn't even let me have a brownie, and I'm starving." Kristy reached for the biscuit tin, so I said, "No. She won't let me eat here, either."

Kristy looked horrified. "Okay," she said. "Then we'll get revenge on her at the sleepover."

Uh-oh.

23rd CHAPTER

Mary Anne

I did not like Mrs Tate. No question about it. But I was not sure I wanted to get revenge on her. I had a feeling that getting revenge was one of Kristy's great ideas that was somehow going to get me in trouble. Just like when we experimented with the washing machine.

But I had no power over Kristy. I would just have to see what happened.

Promptly at six o'clock, our doorbell rang.

"My friends are here!" I called to Mrs Tate. "I'll let them in."

I ran to our front door. There stood Kristy and Claudia. They were each carrying a sleeping bag. Claudia was also carrying an overnight bag. Kristy was wearing a backpack.

"Hi! Come on in," I said.

"We are going straight upstairs—" Kristy started to say.

"Well, now. Let me meet your friends." Mrs Tate had followed me into the hall. "Won't you introduce me, Mary Anne?"

Introduce her? Oh, no. I tried to remember the manners Dad had drilled into me. "Um, Mrs Tate, I am pleased to present," I began, and then forgot the rest of the speech. I started again. "Mrs Tate, I am pleased—I am pleased to present my friends Kristy Thomas and Claudia Kishi. Kristy and Claudia, I am pleased to present my . . . Mrs Tate." (At the last moment, I couldn't bring myself to introduce her as my anything, because I was so cross with her.)

Kristy and Claudia had already begun to giggle over my speech. But Mrs Tate solemnly held out her hand and said, "Pleased to meet you."

Kristy and Claudia shook it, choking back laughter. Then they fled upstairs. I started to follow them, but was called back by Mrs Tate.

"Mary Anne? Did you girls want pizza for dinner?"

"Yes," I said hesitantly.

"Are you going to order one?"

"No, we have frozen ones here. Dad doesn't let us order it."

"Okay. When do you want to eat?"

"In an hour," Kristy yelled from upstairs. I didn't ask her why. I knew she had a reason, and

Claud and I would find it out later.

"Fine," said Mrs Tate. "I'll call you when it's ready. I'm going to eat now, though. Something healthy. I don't approve of pizza."

I finally escaped to my room. As soon as I was inside, Kristy closed the door behind me. "She's *weird*!" she exclaimed.

"What a surprise," I said. "Another weird one."

"Claudia, she wouldn't even let Mary Anne have a brownie when she got home from school," Kristy said indignantly. "She told her she had to eat an apple instead, and that she couldn't eat at my house."

Claudia wrinkled her nose. "Too bad, Mary Anne. You always get the worst babysitters. This one smells like something, too."

"Vinegar?" I suggested.

"Maybe. Yuk."

"Anyway, tonight we are going to get revenge on Mrs Tate," Kristy whispered excitedly. "On account of the brownie."

"Revenge? What are we going to do?" asked Claud.

"Put pepper in her food," said Kristy. She must have been thinking about it all afternoon. She looked pleased with herself.

"Oh, no . . ." I said.

"Come on, Mary Anne. We're doing this for you."

"But I—"

"We just sneak downstairs," Kristy went on, ignoring me. "Then you two distract her, and I'll run into the kitchen, get the pepper, and dump it on her food. Where's the pepper, Mary Anne? I have to know before we start."

"In a blue shaker on the counter by the fridge." See how I kept getting myself into these messes? I could have just told Kristy I didn't know where the pepper was. But no, I played along with her, and before I knew it, I was in trouble.

"Right," said Kristy. "Now—how are you two going to distract her?"

I looked at Claudia. She looked at me. We shrugged.

"Well, it can't be that hard," said Kristy. "Let me see. Okay, you two go into the living room and start shrieking that you see a spider. That always gets old ladies moving. They hate spiders. She'll either want to catch it or kill it, and that could take a few minutes."

"Oh, I don't know," I said, but Kristy had already grabbed my wrist and was pulling me to the door. Claudia was following, looking excited.

We tiptoed down the stairs. At the bottom, Kristy nudged Claudia and me in the direction of the living room. "Go *on*," she whispered urgently.

Claud and I ran forward, and Kristy took a few

226

steps back up the stairs, in case Mrs Tate went to the living room via the hall.

"Spider!" Claud yelled frantically. "Spider!" She elbowed me.

"Um, spider in the living room, Mrs Tate!" I called.

"What kind?" replied Mrs Tate. Her voice came from the kitchen.

What *kind*?

"The brown kind!" yelped Claudia. "Please come and get it. We're scared of it. It looks like it has teeth."

Mrs Tate sauntered into the living room, muttering a stream of things. "No spider has teeth . . . let living creatures be . . . was just about to eat . . . never heard of such—" She paused. "Where *is* it?"

Claudia pretended to peer at the curtains. "Well, it was just here."

"I reckon it's gone," I said.

"Tsk." Mrs Tate returned to the kitchen, and Claud and I flew upstairs. Kristy was on the floor, sitting on her sleeping bag.

"Did you do it?" I asked her.

"Yup. Come on. Let's go and watch."

We crept downstairs again. Kristy paused on the next to last step, and signalled to us to be quiet. Then we peered around the corner into the kitchen. Mrs Tate was seated at the table, facing slightly away from us. Her fork was poised above the plate of salad she'd made. She lowered the fork, stabbed a tomato slice, and put it in her mouth.

"Okay," whispered Kristy. "Now watch . . . now watch."

Not much happened.

Mrs Tate made a face. She chewed a bit more and made a worse face. Then she leaned forward and sniffed at the salad. She sneezed.

"Okay," said Kristy again, sounding even more excited.

But Mrs Tate simply threw away her salad and started making another one.

Kristy frowned. "I don't know. I thought she'd have a fit when she tasted all that pepper."

I was beginning to feel relieved. We had got our revenge without getting in trouble. Now I could relax and enjoy the sleepover.

But Kristy said, "We'll just have to play another joke, that's all. And I know the perfect one. Mary Anne, where's your hammer? We need a hammer and some tacks. Carpet tacks, not drawing pins."

"*Kristy*. What are you going to do?"

"Nail Mrs Tate's slippers to the floor."

"What slippers?"

"Those horrible pink things she left in the hall by the cupboard."

I gave up. Without any arguing, I produced the hammer and some tacks. Kristy did the actual

Mary Anne

nailing. Claudia and I covered up the sound by turning the TV up to top volume. By the time Mrs Tate called to us to turn it down, Kristy had finished her job.

"Now," Kristy whispered as the three of us sat down at the kitchen table to await our pizza, "we just have to watch her when she steps into those slippers. I hope she puts them on soon."

At the time, Mrs Tate was wearing shoes. They squeaked a little as she bustled around the kitchen, slicing the pizza and pouring glasses of juice and milk for my friends and me. After one particularly loud squeak, she said, "Goodness! Excuse me, girls. I think maybe I'll put my slippers on. These shoes are beginning to hurt my feet."

Kristy and Claudia and I glanced at each other. Mrs Tate had just served our food, but we couldn't think about eating it. We gazed into the hall where the slippers sat.

Mrs Tate approached the slippers. She slid first one foot then the other into them. Then she tried to move the first foot forward, stumbled, and put her hand against the wall to steady herself.

"My," she said thoughtfully. She looked in the direction of the kitchen, and Kristy and Claudia and I busied ourselves with our pizza. Out of the corners of our eyes, we saw Mrs Tate bend over to examine the slippers. When she saw the tacks, she

229

just smiled, prised the slippers from the floor, removed the tacks, and put the slippers on.

I was amazed. Mrs Tate had not got angry! She'd seen the tacks and she had actually smiled. She was a very different sort of adult.

Kristy could not wait for us to finish our pizza. When we did (and I might add that Claud had only *just* finished—a piece of crust was still in her mouth), she hurried us upstairs again.

"Let's play another joke!" exclaimed Kristy.

"Yeah, she *liked* the joke, I think," said Claud.

"I can't believe it. An old babysitter who didn't get cross," I added. "Maybe she isn't like the others after all."

Kristy's next trick was to find this incredibly scary rubber mask someone once gave me and hang it inside the refrigerator over the lightbulb. "See, later," Kristy explained to us, "when Mrs Tate opens the fridge that mask will just be hanging there, glowing."

This was exactly what happened. About an hour later Mrs Tate shuffled into the kitchen in her slippers and opened the refrigerator. She hadn't bothered to turn on the kitchen light, so the mask looked especially frightening.

"Good one, girls!" called Mrs Tate cheerfully.

"Thanks!" Kristy called back. We'd been watching from the dining room. We weren't even trying to hide any more.

"You're very creative," Mrs Tate added.

Well, that did it. We couldn't get enough of the game. And now Claudia and I pitched in much more willingly. We thought up joke after joke. By eleven o'clock, we were hysterical. All four of us. And Mrs Tate had told us about a very wonderful practical joke—spreading cling film over a toilet bowl so lightly that when someone sits down they don't know it's there and, well, you can imagine the rest.

I learned three good lessons that night. One, it was okay to do silly, crazy things every now and then. Just because Dad was cautious and careful and formal all the time, I didn't have to be. Two, most people (like Mrs Tate) have a good sense of humour and appreciate humour in others. I remembered that when I began babysitting myself a few years later. Now I always try to keep my sense of humour intact when I'm around kids. It makes my job much easier, and the kids feel more relaxed. Three, you shouldn't judge people by their appearances. Mrs Tate may have looked like all those other old ladies from the agency, but she sure didn't act like them.

If I had had any doubts about that last lesson when I went to bed that night, I didn't when I woke up the next morning. Claudia and Kristy and I ran downstairs and found Mrs Tate stirring a big pot of something on the stove.

"Breakfast!" said Mrs Tate.

My friends and I crowded around the pot and

231

peered inside. We saw a stew of old socks, a tennis ball, several bottle caps, and some vegetable peel in water.

We dissolved in laughter.

"She got us!" exclaimed Kristy with admiration. "An adult got us!"

What I Did this Summer
by Kristy Thomas

This summer I did a lot of baby-sitting. My friend Bart and I coached a couple of softball teams for little kids. My friend Mary Anne and I took a marathon bike ride. And my little brother and I went fishing with our stepfather. We didn't catch much, but we had fun. Best of all, my friends and I had a slumber party, and we ended up taking a trip down memory lane. Someone

Kristy

suggested that we each try to decide on our most vivid memory. This was harder than it sounded. But, boy, the memories that came up—divorces, crises, new babies, ~~epff apff~~ epiphanies..

Epiphany. I like that word. Maybe this one-page essay wasn't such a bad idea after all. It made me try to put the summer in perspective, and do it concisely; to pare it down to bare bones and analyse it. That in itself was a small epiphany—the realization that the assignment was more meaningful than I'd thought. So was my memory of the day I realized I could be a capable person and use that talent well. Another small epiphany.

I think all of us SMS students used our vivid memories in some way in our essays. We talked about that one night, the very last night in August, just a few days before school would begin again. We had gathered at my house for another slumber party—Mary Anne, Jessi, Shannon, Mallory, Stacey, Claudia, and I. And of course we talked about that last slumber party.

"What a question you asked, Jessi," said Stacey. "I've been dredging up memories all summer."

234

"I'm sorry," said Jessi.

"No, no. I think it's a good thing. Just because a memory is painful doesn't mean it's bad. I like taking out all of my old memories and looking at them. It's like going through a photo album."

"Yeah," agreed Mal. "You see faces you haven't seen in a long time, and maybe some of the people are dead now, or they've moved away, but you still like looking at them and remembering the good times."

"But Stacey's talking about remembering the *bad* times," spoke up Mary Anne. "Weren't you, Stace? And I know what you mean. You find an old memory, one that's not so pleasant, and you examine it, and you see what you've learned from it, or how it helped you."

"You also see that you lived through it, as bad as it was," said Shannon. "That might be the most important thing. You survived. And you're probably a stronger person for it."

"Well, anyway, not all of our memories were so bad or serious," I said. "Look at Mary Anne's. I can't believe we actually nailed Mrs Tate's slippers to the floor. Boy, just think if one of our sitting charges ever did that to *us*. What would we do?"

"Probably laugh, thanks to Mrs Tate," said Mary Anne.

"Shannon, your story was incredible," Jessi

235

spoke up. "Whatever happened to Sally White anyway?"

"She moved away at the end of the school year. I hadn't thought about her much until after our slumber party. But I'm glad I did. I know my essay is good. It's very heartfelt, but I had enough distance to write about it without being all sloppy and over-emotional."

Claudia cleared her throat. "This conversation is beginning to sound like an English lesson. Can we please change the subject?"

"To what?" I asked.

But the phone rang before she could answer me.

"Hello, Kristy?" said a familiar voice.

"Dawn!" I shrieked.

Everyone else began to shriek, too. I passed the phone around from one person to another. When it was finally passed back to me, Dawn said, "I miss you all so much. I just had to call during your party. You know what I was thinking about just now? I was thinking about another question. What was the most exciting day of your life?"

What was the most *exciting* day of my life? Hmm . . .